A MESSAGE FROM CHICKEN HOUSE

I've always believed in (my fellow!) little people. Often hidden, they help us in small but important ways – and they're always there when things get too tough. In legend, little people are forever a connection to other worlds . . . and that's the case in this extraordinary story too. Pádraig gives heart and soul, danger and excitement to what happens when children need help the most.

BARRY CUNNINGHAM
Publisher
Chicken House

PÁDRAIG KENNY

Chicken House

2 Palmer Street, Frome, Somerset BA11 1DS
www.chickenhousebooks.com

Text © Pádraig Kenny 2019
Illustration © Jane Newland 2019

First published in Great Britain in 2019
Chicken House
2 Palmer Street
Frome, Somerset BA11 1DS
United Kingdom
www.chickenhousebooks.com

Cover and interior design by Helen Crawford-White
Typeset by Dorchester Typesetting Group Ltd
Printed and bound in Great Britain by CPI Group (UK) Ltd, Croydon, CR0 4YY

The paper used in this Chicken House book is made
from wood grown in sustainable forests.

1 3 5 7 9 10 8 6 4 2

British Library Cataloguing in Publication data available.

ISBN 978-1-911490-39-5
eISBN 978-1-912626-01-4

For my parents

Also by Pádraig Kenny
Tin

PROLOGUE

I t was night when Pog heard weeping in the forest.

He'd been patrolling for an hour, and the only sounds had been the occasional cries of foxes, or the low hooting of owls.

Pog sniffed the air. There was a scent.

Human scent.

Pog followed the smell. He skipped over tree roots, his eyes finely attuned to the night, his furry ears twitching as he got closer to the sound. It was coming from the trees encircling the dark forbidden heart of the forest. Pog's hackles immediately stood on end. He paced back and forth fretfully, listening to the weeping before plunging into the undergrowth.

Pog peeked out from behind a bush and into the circular clearing which was dotted with stunted tree trunks. There was a human child sitting on one of the old stumps. A girl with dark curly hair. She was sobbing inconsolably into her hands. Pog recognized her instantly and nodded in understanding. He'd already seen her with the tall ones that very morning. They'd arrived at the house in their metal box on wheels.

This was something entirely new for Pog. He was used to protecting and patrolling, not coming across the children of tall ones crying in the forest. He didn't know what to do. He didn't want to reveal himself, but the girl was clearly lost. *What to do? What to do?* he thought, chewing on his thumb.

The decision was made for him as he saw the girl suddenly look up towards the ancient twisted tree that lay at the centre of the clearing. It was as if she'd heard something. She stood up, frowning curiously at the tree, and then started to walk carefully towards it.

'Pssst! No!' Pog hissed, drawing his sword and staff without thinking.

The girl wheeled round. 'Who's that? Who's there?'

Pog hid behind the bush, his chest tight, muscles tensed.

'A friend,' he said. 'Is you lost?'

The girl wiped her eyes and nodded. 'Yes,' she whimpered.

'Come then, and Pog will show you the way home.'

The girl hunched her shoulders and didn't move. Behind her, a sliver of moonlight shone on the tree, and the black bark rippled for a moment, as if a

serpent were twisting beneath it. Pog smelt something fetid and rotten. He licked his lips. He needed
to get the girl away from the tree, but he couldn't
reveal himself. It was forbidden.

'Come now,' he said, trying to keep his tone light
and friendly.

The girl clutched her hands to her chest and
retreated a couple of steps closer to the tree. Pog saw
that supple insidious movement again beneath the
skin of the tree, and he fancied he heard a hissing
whisper. The girl was frightened, and hiding from
her was only making things worse. There was only
one thing for it.

Pog stepped into the clearing.

The girl blinked in disbelief. 'Who are you?' she
asked, her lower lip trembling.

'Pog Lumpkin. A friend.' Pog smiled at the girl to
show her he meant no harm. The warmth he felt
when she smiled in response was a surprise to him.

'You're all furry,' said the girl.

'Pog is of the First Folk. We's all furry. Not like
you tall folk.' He beckoned the girl forward, smiling
at her while keeping one eye on the tree. 'Pog will
show you the way home. Come, follow Pog.'

As the girl came towards him, Pog sighed
inwardly with relief. He cast one eye over his shoul-

der as they left the clearing behind. Pog thought he heard that whisper again, but perhaps it was his imagination. The tree was still, but its bark had a reptilian sheen.

Clouds cleared and the moon came out and lit their way. Pog bounded through the forest, the girl keeping pace with him. Pog started to speed up and the girl laughed as she chased after him. Pog laughed too, but he took care not to go too fast in case he lost her.

It didn't take them long to reach the large house that lay at the edge of the forest. Pog and the girl went up the driveway and stopped outside the front door. There was a light on in one of the windows.

'There now,' he said.

The girl smiled down at him. 'Thank you, Pog.'

Pog felt strange. There was a fluttering in his chest. No one had spoken his name in years.

'Pog must go now.'

'Will I see you again?' asked the girl.

'Maybe,' said Pog.

'Are you alone?'

The question took Pog by surprise. He felt an ache in his throat. He shook his head. 'Not now,' he smiled.

The girl waved goodbye and Pog slipped around

the corner of the house, and watched as she knocked on the door. A tall man with grey hair opened the door. He and the girl embraced, and the sight of it made Pog feel sad and happy at the same time.

They both went inside and Pog felt almost disappointed as the door closed.

He shimmied up the drainpipe and squeezed in through the hole that led into the attic. Pog landed deftly on the attic floor and started to remove his sword and staff.

Are you alone? Pog thought about the question. Yes, he had been. He had been alone in the dark for a very long time, but he wasn't alone now.

But what Pog didn't know was that in two weeks' time the girl would be gone. Her grandparents would soon follow, and the house would be empty. And there Pog would stay in the attic, patrolling at night, keeping to a long-held promise. And spring would come, summers would pass, many autumns, many winters. It would just be Pog then, alone in the dark, for what seemed like for ever.

Until they came.

PART 1

Pog in the Dark

CHAPTER 1

30 YEARS LATER

'Your mum's in Ipswich.'

Penny looked up from unpacking a box of books to see her dad waggling his phone at her.

'Ipswich,' he said again, and he shook his head and gave a sheepish smile.

Penny felt her cheeks get hot and she looked across the hallway towards David who was unpacking another box only a metre or so away from her. She wanted him to look up at her, so that she could have someone to share her irritation with, but David's head was bent low. It was obvious that he didn't want to have anything to do with the situation.

Penny turned back towards her dad. He seemed

to be waiting for her to say something. She rubbed her forehead vigorously and just said, 'Right.'

Her dad smiled apologetically. Penny hated that smile.

'Bit of confusion about directions.' He shrugged. 'She should be here after lunch.'

Penny cleared her throat. She didn't know what he expected her to say. He grinned and waggled his phone again and put it in his pocket. Penny fought the urge to roll her eyes. Instead, she remembered herself and she did what she'd been doing for the past three months. She flashed one of her best brilliant smiles. 'That's good, Dad,' she said.

Her dad seemed encouraged by this, and for a moment he seemed to stand that little bit taller, like a child who'd just been complimented by a parent. Penny felt a pang of guilt for feeling so irritated in the first place. After all, he was only trying his best. They were all trying their best.

'Did you hear that, David? Mum will be here after lunch.'

David said nothing and just kept unpacking.

Penny looked at the boxes that were scattered around the hall. Their whole lives were squeezed in them, waiting to be unpacked in their new home. For a moment Penny wondered if they could just leave the boxes as they were and not unpack anything. That way they could just stay as they were, not moving forward, not moving back, stuck in time where things might be safer. Stuck between the awful past and an equally awful future.

'Maybe you could both go outside and explore for a bit,' said Dad.

'Whatever,' David said, shrugging his shoulders.

Sometimes Penny wondered if he was the one who had just become a teenager and not her. When Penny looked into his eyes he seemed to be the oldest-looking eleven-year-old in the world.

'Look at it. The state of it. I wouldn't let a dog live in it,' David growled.

He was kicking gravel on the driveway, his hands deep in his pockets.

Penny looked at the rickety house looming above them. He had a point. No one had lived here for decades. It had belonged to their mum's grandparents, and they'd passed it on to Mum. It was coming apart at the seams, and their mum had never had the time to do anything about it. But even though the house was sloppy and angular, Penny liked it. Her dad's plan was to apply his architectural skills and do it up. Penny and David

11

thought he was mad. It would have been easier to stay in London, but looking at the house now, Penny was beginning to understand in some small way what their father was about. It would take a lot of work, but maybe it would be good for him, good for them all.

'Bet there's rats up there. Rats and all sorts of things.' David was looking at the roof. 'Look how many holes are up there. That's how they get in. Rats can climb anything.'

Penny looked up and squinted her eyes.

'And loose slates for the rain. Bet it's like a swamp up there. Pools of water for the rats to drink, and maggots, and . . . and . . .' David kicked a stone and it went skidding into a bush.

There was silence for a few moments. Penny felt the breeze on her face and it rippled through her brown curls. She could smell wood and leaves on the air.

'Let's go for a walk in the forest,' she said.

She was surprised when David didn't complain about her suggestion. They walked down the drive-way together, their shoes crunching on the gravel. David insisted on dragging his feet. Penny fought the urge to tell him to stop. That would only risk more sulks from him, and she was determined to lighten the mood. She decided that a walk through trees and sunlight would do them both the power of good.

They crossed the dirt road – a quiet, narrow track at the end of the drive. It was a bright, warm summer's day, and the shade looked particularly inviting. The house was bounded on all sides by forest, although the trees were thicker and deeper on the side across the road. The nearest village was eight miles away. Penny liked the way it all felt; isolated, away from anyone who could remind them of the bustle of the outside world.

They entered the forest and the hush settled around them. They picked their way through trees and rocks without saying a word, following a well-worn track to avoid getting lost. After about twenty minutes, they found themselves in a part of the forest where the trees seemed even more densely packed. They both stood still and just looked at the trees and listened to the wind hiss through the leaves.

Penny saw David frown. 'What is it?' she asked.

'Do you hear that?' said David.

Penny listened hard, but there was no sound at all apart from the wind in the trees.

David pointed at the clump of trees. 'It came from in there.'

Penny looked at the trees. They were gnarled and twisted together. They looked almost as if they were whispering to each other.

David took a step forward.

'David!'

David scowled at her. 'What?'

'Don't go in there.'

'Why? Are you afraid there might be monsters?'

He was sneering, but Penny could see the flicker of doubt in his eyes. There was something in there. He felt it too.

'Come on,' said Penny, 'we should get back.'

She was glad to walk away from that place. She noticed David kept looking over his shoulder as they headed back.

'We're in the middle of nowhere,' David said, still looking back to where they'd just come from.

'This is a forest,' said Penny. 'It's not nowhere.'

David curled his lip in disdain. 'It's not anywhere, Pen.'

Penny breathed in the warm, clean air. Maybe it wouldn't be so bad. Maybe they were better off out of London. Peace was probably what they needed. Penny had been anxious and a little frightened by the idea of coming up here to Allbridge, but now she didn't feel so scared. *It's for the best*, she kept telling herself. *It's for the best.*

She said the next words without even thinking. It was only afterwards, when they were back at the house, that she would realize that she had sounded just like Dad.

'Mum will like it here,' she said brightly.

David shook his head and said something without turning around. Penny pretended she hadn't heard him. They walked back in silence.

The silence remained all through the afternoon as they continued to unpack boxes.

Penny was putting some books in a bookcase in the sitting room when noise from outside caught her attention.

She looked out the window to see a van pull into the driveway. The driver got out. He was dressed in grey overalls with the removal company's logo over his left pocket. He went to the back of the van, opened the door, and took out a box which he cradled under his right arm. He closed the van doors and headed for the house.

Penny bolted out of the sitting room, kicking a box on her way, sending it skidding across the hallway. David gave her a reproachful look, but she was too busy trying to get to the door to notice it. The delivery man knocked on the door, and Penny shouted, 'I'll get it.'

She opened the door. The delivery man grinned at her, and looked at his clipboard. 'Cresswells, yeah?'

Penny didn't like his tone – he was too casual, too friendly. It seemed inappropriate. She nodded.

'Sorry about the delay; it was just that there was a bit of confusion and it got put in the van. I know you'd marked it as a personal item, but we had a new lad and he doesn't know procedure.'

The man in the overalls shrugged and smiled. Penny clenched her jaw.

'Didn't even bother himself to check our labelling system, so he packed it. The gaffer has had a few words with him already.' The man chuckled. 'He won't be doing that again in a hurry.' He started clucking with his tongue while reading the note on his clipboard. 'Says here it was headed for storage. Just as well you rang—'

Penny reached out her hands. 'Right, yeah, can you just give me my mum, please?'

The delivery man looked surprised and he grinned at what he thought was a joke. Then he saw the look in Penny's eyes, and his grin started to crumple. He took half a step back.

'What?'

'Can you just give her to me, please?'

Penny's tone was brisk, edging just a little bit towards anger. The man's smile vanished completely, and he eyed her warily as he handed over the box. Penny snatched it away from him.

'You'll have to sign,' he said, almost leaning away from her as he handed her the clipboard.

Penny signed the form and slammed the door without even waiting for the delivery man to say his goodbyes. She turned around to find both David and Dad looking at her. She raised the box up slightly.

'She came,' she said.

No one said anything for a moment, then Dad stepped forward. Penny handed him the box.

Dad jerked his head in the direction of the sitting room. Penny nodded, and she and David followed him in. Dad put the box on the floor and opened it. He gently pushed aside the packing straw and tenderly took out the bronze urn it contained. Dad stood up and walked towards the fireplace. He put the urn on the mantelpiece and took a few steps back.

'What do you think?' he said.

Penny and David weren't sure what to say.

'Do you think she'll be happy here?' asked Dad.

No one said anything, until finally Penny couldn't take it any more and she just said, 'Yes.'

'I do too,' said Dad. 'I do too.'

For a minute or two he gave a little agitated shuffle as if he wasn't sure how to stand. He crossed and uncrossed his arms. He scratched the hair on his chin and rubbed his lower lip with his thumb. During all of this he kept his eyes on the urn. Eventually he turned and left the room without looking at them, as if he'd forgotten they were there at all.

After a while Penny turned around to see that David was gone too. She stepped towards the fireplace and held her hand out towards the urn. She touched the cool surface and remembered the words David had spoken in the forest. The words she'd chosen to ignore:

Mum's dead.

CHAPTER 2

Pog listened and Pog waited above in the attic. When darkness came he knew the humans were asleep. He could tell because the house was quiet and all he could hear was the tall one's and two not-so-tall-ones' regular breathing. Tall ones were always sleeping when it got dark. Grandfa told him it was because they were afraid of the dark and couldn't see very well in it, not like First Folk could. Not like Pog.

Pog stood up straight, his ears twitching, holding his breath. He'd sensed them even before they'd arrived at the house. It was like a special pressure in the air, or a cloud rolling in from far away, soft and smooth, but dark. No one had come to the house for a long time, not for many years.

Pog prepared himself. He sheathed his sword in

its scabbard, clipped his rope and grappling hook to his belt, and took his staff from where it leant against the wall. Pog smiled as he gazed upon the staff. Grandfa's staff, handed down to him as it always had been handed down, Lumpkin to Lump-kin, from generation to generation. Looking at it never ceased to fill him with pride. It was made from black wood, its length covered in carved whorls and glyphs.

Pog strapped the staff to his back and raised himself up to his full height, which was probably no more than two feet. With Grandfa's staff on his person he was more than just a simple forest dweller. He was Pog Lumpkin of the Burrows to the North, before the Far Reaches, Keeper of the Necessary, Guardian against the Dark, Pog of the First Folk.

Grandfa would be proud, he thought, then the voice inside his head corrected him.

Grandfa is proud, Pog.

Pog looked up into the dark and smiled. He took in a deep breath and his chest ballooned at the sound of his grandfa's voice.

But there was another voice now. Sly, insidious.

But Grandfa is gone, Pog. All are gone. Many years now, Pog. Pog is alone.

Pog felt his throat tighten, and his eyes stung.

'Hush now,' he whispered, 'Pog has things to be getting on with. None of this nonsense now.'

He had to ensure that the Necessary was locked.

He lifted the attic door – soft as you like, with barely an effort – and down he went, swinging himself from the lip of the opening, letting go, and tumbling over and over until he landed with a muffled thump on the landing.

He was nervous, and yet there was a lightness in his chest, a tingling sense of giddiness that seemed to creep upwards and tickle his throat. Pog didn't understand this strange excitement. He supposed it might be exciting because this felt like an adventure of sorts, now that the tall ones were here.

He crouched for a moment and twitched his ears. His broad, flat nose snuffled as he sniffed the air. Nothing in the darkness, just low soft breaths, the sound of tall folk dreaming.

Pog wondered what they dreamt of as he padded through the dark. He dreamt lots, mainly of Grandfa and the Burrows and the time before he had been entrusted with his task. Most of the time he didn't want to wake from such dreams. The ache he felt when he did wake seemed to be deep within his bones. He could hear Grandfa's voice even now as he crept along the landing.

Good Pog. Silent Pog.

Pog smiled to himself and thanked his grandfa.

Careful now, Pog, said Grandfa. *Things are in the dark. Always be keeping careful.*

Pog nodded and said he would be just that.

Pog passed a bedroom door. The girl was in there. He could hear her breathing, soft and low. He padded past the next room. The boy was in this one, but his breathing was slightly ragged, and Pog thought he heard a whimper. He'd watched them closely from the roof when they'd first arrived. The boy had stood by the girl's side when they had looked up at the house for the first time. The girl was talking and smiling, the boy was just looking sullenly at the house.

Then the bigger tall one had arrived. He had hair on his face, which confused Pog. Why have hair just on your face and head? He thought the tall one looked silly. Having hair all over your body was the most natural thing in the world. Pog thought that having some just on your face and head was very strange indeed.

Pog reached the top of the stairs and hopped up on to the banister. He slid right down, swift and silent, and landed in the hallway between some boxes. He ambled around and started sniffing each box. They were full of things that only tall folk had use for. Metal things, and soft fluffy things, and plates and dishes with pictures on them. *Why would you have pictures on something you were eating off?* Pog thought. Pog had never seen so many strange objects, not since the old tall folk who had lived here once. They'd left and taken everything with them. These new visitors had so many things. Books too – they had lots of those. Some of them were bigger than Pog and had pictures on the front of tall-folk buildings and great steel bridges. Pog flitted between each box, sniffing them and pawing quickly through their contents. *Where to start?* he wondered.

He heard a sound.

Pog whipped his head round and his hand went to his sword. The sound had come from the room to his right. He tensed and pressed himself up against the side of a box.

Pay attention, Pog.

Pog cursed himself for being so lax. The sound came again. It sounded like someone clearing their throat.

He let a few moments pass before looking out from behind the box. The door of the room the sound had come from was slightly ajar. There was a dim light coming from the room. Pog shook his head at his own foolishness, and he could almost hear Grandfa tutting in disapproval.

Pog crept towards the door. He peered through the gap.

The man was sitting on a couch with his back to the door. He was hunched over, and Pog thought there was something strange about the way he was sitting. Then Pog noticed the man's shoulders were going up and down, and he was making strange sounds.

Pog realized the man was crying.

For a moment Pog was so surprised he couldn't move.

He shook himself and, taking advantage of the man's distressed state, rolled into the room and behind the couch. Pog was fascinated now. He wondered why the man was so upset.

The man continued sobbing for a while, until his crying became little more than sniffles. He started to mutter things to himself. Pog heard the word 'stupid' used quite a lot. Who was he talking to? There was no one else in the room. The whole thing was very confusing. Mouse poked his nose out from a crack in the skirting board and looked at Pog curiously. Pog put a finger to his lips and winked at him.

After a few minutes Pog felt the couch shift as the man stood up. There was a great honking sound which almost made Pog jump out of his pelt, then the man headed towards the door.

The light went out, and Pog heard the door close.

He waited a few moments before coming out of hiding. He crept around the couch to where the man had been sitting. There was a low table in front of the couch, and on the table was a selection of books, including one very large one which lay open.

Pog hopped up on to the table and peered at the book. He flinched for a moment and shied away from it, but then plucked up the courage to peer at it again. What he saw amazed him. The book was filled with pictures of the man and the two children, and there was a woman with them. The pictures looked real, as if the tall folk had been taken from real life and put on the page, but lots and lots of times. Pog blinked and tentatively reached out and touched one of the pictures. He exhaled in wonder, and he spotted Mouse by the couch now, nibbling on a crumb. Pog scratched his head.

'It's a mystery, Mouse, and no mistake.'

Pog turned back to the pictures. The smaller tall

folk were in lots of them, but there were others in which the man and the woman appeared. In all of them the tall folk were smiling. There was one in which the woman sat on a couch with the boy on her right and the girl on her left. She had her arms around both of them. Pog noticed that the woman had curls just like the girl, but that she seemed to be a mixture of the boy and the girl. Her green eyes shone, and so did those of the children. Pog frowned. Both the boy and the girl looked different now to the way they looked in the pictures. He couldn't tell exactly how, but he knew they somehow looked the same but changed. How could that be? Looking the same, yet not?

Pog looked more closely at the picture. The woman and the girl looked alike. There was something about them both that made him frown all the more. They seemed strangely familiar to him. Pog's lips moved soundlessly, as if he was trying to translate their images. They weren't like the tall ones who had originally lived here. The old man and old woman had never ventured out much. They sat in most days and did what they called 'cross words'. Pog had no idea what this was. These tall folk were different. There was something sad about them, as if they were all burdened by a terrible weight. Pog also wondered why the woman wasn't here. It was all very curious.

There were lots of empty bookcases up against the walls of the room. Pog leapt off the table and walked towards one. He looked at it while scratching his chin, then he turned and walked to the door. For a moment he stopped and looked back at the books. He frowned, then shrugged and left the room. He had his duty to attend to. Pog crept down the hallway and headed to the back of the house to the Necessary.

Pog smirked to himself as he felt the tingle of air at the end of the hallway. There was an enchantment laid here. Deep and powerful. One that the tall folk had never suspected. It was an enchantment so strong they had even built their house around it without knowing.

He reached the door at the end of the hallway and laid his right palm down on the wood. He looked at the symbol that had been inscribed in blue dye near the base of the door. Pog closed his eyes and concentrated. His lips curled up slightly in the ghost of a smile, then he placed his left cheek against the door and felt the low steady thrum in his bones.

The Necessary was fixed. Pog could feel it. Locked and scissioned.

Pog stood away from the door and sighed with satisfaction, then with a quick twirl of his staff he headed for the stairs.

He was at the bottom of the stairs when he felt the slight prickle on the back of his neck. He turned to look at the door to the study. He could hear Mouse scurrying in there. Pog debated with himself for a moment. He had a strange thought. Maybe there was something he could do to help the tall folk. Moving somewhere that wasn't home wasn't an easy thing to do. Pog knew what that felt like. He mulled it over for a moment. He finally gave a rueful smile and shook his head as if he was a tiny bit exasperated with himself.

'Best be quick and about it so, Pog,' he said to himself.

Pog headed back towards the room.

It took him some time to accomplish his task. When he was finished he felt satisfied and had to resist the urge to whistle a jaunty tune as he made his way back upstairs.

Inside the attic he divested himself of his sword, but kept his staff. He crept into his den, a ramshackle heap of old blankets, paper and bits of wood in a corner, and he lay down.

He placed the staff by his side and gently traced

the whorls with his finger.

Pog felt a sudden great weight on his chest. He closed his eyes tight, tight as could be, and he eventually drifted off to sleep.

In his dreams, Pog travelled. Pog went back.

He was by a stream. The sun was shining. He was holding his fishing rod, and he could feel the weight lift from his chest because he knew that he would turn and Grandfa would be standing there beside him.

And there he was, not much taller than Pog, but stocky and big-boned.

This was the day Grandfa had taught him how to fish.

Grandfa smiled at him, and Pog felt a warmth that was like being swept up in a great big wave.

'Pay attention now, Pog,' said Grandfa, his mouth clamped around his pipe.

'Pog will,' said Pog.

Grandfa smiled at him, and Pog thought in that moment that his heart would burst with happiness.

'Always be paying attention,' said Grandfa, and Pog mouthed the same words just as Grandfa spoke them.

In the attic, in the world outside his dreams, a sleeping Pog smiled.

And a single tear rolled down his cheek.

CHAPTER 3

David sat bolt upright in bed, gasping for breath.

For one panicked moment he could still feel that sensation of something cold and wet pressing in around him, tight to his chest, forcing its way down his throat, until he had to struggle for air.

David leant over the side of the bed, the blanket bunched tight in his fist, as he kept gasping. He couldn't remember the dream exactly, just that terrible drowning sensation. And the voice ...

David straightened himself up and took in deep breaths, letting them in and out slowly until finally he felt calm enough to look around him.

The room was silvered by the pale moonlight that shone in through his window. The window was almost floor-length, and it didn't have any curtains yet. It made him feel exposed.

He closed his eyes and tried to calm himself that bit more. It was then that he heard a creaking sound just outside his door. He opened his eyes and listened.

Something was close by. He could sense it.

'Who's there?' he whispered. He rolled over and looked at the door. He held his breath.

It had come from outside his room. He was sure of it.

Mustering all his willpower, David moved his legs and slid them out of the bed. He swallowed hard as he looked at the door.

Just open it, he thought. *It's probably nothing.*

He lowered his legs off the bed, and his bare feet touched the floorboards.

David crept towards the door. He reached a hand out and wrapped it around the doorknob. It was one of those old brass ones, and it wobbled in its setting. He held it with two hands to compensate for its shakiness, and he turned it. Slowly.

His throat was dry, and he licked his lips as the knob turned. There was a barely audible creak, but it was a sound that went on too long for his liking, and David tried to combat it by opening the door swiftly and smoothly. He opened the door fully.

He half expected something to crash in on top of

31

him – something huge and dark – and he hunched his shoulders in fear and expectation, but there was nothing out there.

David stepped out into the hall. He looked left and right, and listened.

There was nothing, not a sound.

David wasn't convinced. He knew he'd heard something.

'Hello?' he said to the dark. When the dark didn't answer he said, 'Hello?' again, feeling stupid. The back of his neck tingled. He had the peculiar sensation that he was being watched.

After a few moments of straining to listen, he sighed and turned to go back into his room.

That was when something scampered past.

David wheeled around, his heart pounding. He was just in time to see something dark and many-legged scuttle down the stairs.

For a moment he couldn't breathe, then he bolted after it.

He got to the top of the stairs just in time to catch a glimpse of something disappear round a corner. He strained his ears and listened. He thought he heard scampering again, but he couldn't be sure. He debated about whether to follow whatever it was, but it was dark down there, and now he was shaking, and he could feel his heart just thumping faster and faster.

He went back into the room, closing the door behind him. He got back into bed and pulled the blanket up to his chin. His chest was tight, and he allowed his breathing to return to normal as he focused on the ceiling. There was only a slight improvement. His shoulders were still tensed, and now he gripped the blanket with two hands. He decided that what he'd seen was a rat. It had to be. After all, it was larger than a mouse.

But it had too many legs, he thought.

As his breathing and his heart slowed, David eventually remembered what had woken him in the first place.

He'd been dreaming about the dark part of the forest, the part that had so unnerved him and Penny. In his dream it was night, and he was alone. There was the stench of something decaying on the air. He was just about to plunge into the trees.

He hadn't told Penny the full truth about their experience in the forest. He hadn't told her what he'd heard, because he was afraid she would think he'd gone mad.

He'd heard it in his dream too, and it was clearer now, more insistent.

It was the sound of someone's voice.

And that voice had been calling his name.

CHAPTER 4

'Right, own up. Which one of you was it?'

Penny looked up from the grey watery gloop that her dad proudly called his 'special super-duper porridge' to see him grinning at her and David across the kitchen table. His grin was a bit too manic for her liking. It was the kind of grin that made his eyes look wide and desperate, as if he was trying too hard to play the happy-go-lucky parent.

'Which one of us was what, Dad?' asked Penny.

Dad looked at her and at David and back again. He wagged his finger at them. 'You two,' he said, chuckling and shaking his head.

'Us two what?' said David. *A little too irritably*, thought Penny.

'The books,' Dad said.

Penny and David looked at each other.

'The books,' Dad said again, as if it was obvious what he was referring to.

Penny and David both frowned at him.

Dad folded his arms and leant back in his chair. 'It was one of you, or both of you. Come on, confess.'

David sighed impatiently and stirred his porridge. Penny hated it when he sighed like that.

'It wasn't us,' she said.

Her dad raised an eyebrow.

Penny shook her head. 'We don't even know what you mean by *the books*.'

Dad smiled again. 'You two,' he said, and he chuckled again and started to clear up some breakfast things.

When her dad turned his back to go towards the sink, Penny looked at David again. David scowled as if to say, 'What are you looking at me for?' and went back to prodding his so-called porridge with the tip of his spoon.

'He did it,' said David.

He and Penny were standing in the room that their dad had designated as his study. The bookshelves were packed with books. The empty boxes were stacked neatly in the hallway.

Penny was bemused. 'Why would he say we did it?'

David gave a half-hearted shrug. 'I dunno.'

Penny narrowed her eyes. 'Are you sure you didn't do it?'

David snorted. 'Why would I do that?'

'I don't know. Maybe to help cheer him up,' said Penny.

David whooped in derision. 'Cheer him up. Mr Smiley Happy Pants. Why would he need cheering up? Have you seen him lately?'

Penny turned away from David so she wouldn't have to look at him. His face was a mixture of anger and resentment. Seeing him like this only made her angry too, and she knew that wouldn't help anybody. She breathed out in an effort to relax.

'You did a very good job, whichever one of you did it,' she said.

David groaned and left the room.

Penny walked over to the coffee table where the family album lay open. The first thing she saw was a photo of the four of them, squinting into the sun. Only Mum had her eyes open, and even in the photo Penny could see their fierce greenness. They were all standing in their old back garden.

Back at home, she thought to herself. She looked around her. This wasn't home.

CHAPTER
5

Once, when David was seven, they'd all gone on a day trip to the British Museum: him, Penny, Dad and Mum. He'd got separated from the others, but he knew his way back to the main entrance. He waited there because he knew they'd come looking for him and it would be one of the first places they'd look. David was calm. He didn't need to tell anyone he was lost; he just waited. Sure enough, half an hour later he heard a familiar voice. He turned to see his mum running towards him, her arms outstretched, calling his name . . .

David stopped. He'd been walking for a while, concentrating on the rhythm of his legs, but now he could feel the tears coming. He simply refused to cry. He wouldn't let that happen. He screwed his eyes shut, and rubbed his hands vigorously against his scalp. He breathed in and out and tried to concentrate on his surroundings. He listened to the breeze through the branches, and looked at the ground, the brown earth mixed with green, the stubbly grass and moss ruffling gently. Calm returned. His mind became still and his limbs relaxed. He concentrated on where he was now, forgetting the past.

That was when he heard it.

There was a soft exhalation, like someone letting out a calm deep breath. The forest darkened slightly as if a great cloud had passed overhead, and yet the sky still seemed to be the same dull grey it had been when he'd entered the forest. The sound seemed to come from the side and pass through him, almost tickling his ears. David jumped up with fright and looked around.

'Who's there?' he shouted.

The soft breath faded on the wind.

David's attention was drawn back to where he thought the sound had originated. The forest was darker there, the trees more densely packed, and they looked different, their bark drier than those of the other trees in the forest, and they looked a deeper shade of brown, almost blackish. It was the place from before, the same place where he and Penny had turned back.

David swallowed; he started forward, his legs as numb as if they belonged to somebody else. The light began to fade, and he felt as if he was not just heading towards a destination, but also moving backwards in time. Sounds became more muffled, and the air had a boggy, swampy taint to it. It tasted dirty and old, like something that had been soured. David was frightened – sweat started to roll down the small of his back – but he kept walking.

And then suddenly the trees opened into a circular clearing. The interlacing branches overhead formed a canopy through which only the tiniest amount of grey light seeped in.

The soil in the clearing was dark and wet. The stunted remains of rotted trunks dotted the area, and in the centre was a tree, black and twisted and ancient. It leant back as if it were trying to stand in the teeth of a hurricane. Its branches were bare, but bulged and knotted in places, like arthritic knuckles. It looked like a thing in pain, and David felt a strange mixture of pity and horror.

He reached a hand round and rubbed the small of his back. There was moisture in the air, but despite this David licked his parched lips. No birds sang here, no breeze was blowing, but David felt a soft susurration beneath everything, and beneath that still, a low tormented groaning that seemed to emanate from the tree.

He stepped towards it, still feeling that strange mixture of pity and revulsion. The closer he got to the tree, the more it seemed to be groaning in pain, and despite his unease David felt compelled to raise his hand. He wanted to touch the tree, to calm it like one would an animal in pain. Besides, it had called to him. He knew that whispering voice from somewhere. It was familiar. He couldn't place it, but he knew if he could focus hard enough, he would remember who it belonged to. It was just a matter of—

David screamed as a sudden burning pain ripped through the centre of his palm and up to his wrist, hot and wet and red.

He'd been so busy thinking about the voice that he hadn't realized he'd touched the tree. He grabbed his right hand with his left. Tears of pain stung his eyes, and he fell to his knees. He squeezed the tears out between closed eyes, and he started to retch with the pain.

He didn't know how long he stayed like that. He'd have gladly collapsed face down in the dirt and stayed there for hours, but the voice wouldn't let him.

'*Shhhhh,*' it said. '*Shhhhh.*' But not in words: more as a soft breeze gently rattling the branches of the surrounding trees. A delicate hiss that was comforting and, again, familiar.

David opened his eyes. His right hand was clenched into a fist. He slowly uncurled his fingers.

The wound was a lot smaller than the pain had suggested it would be. If anything it was just a small gash that didn't even look that deep. And yet the agony he'd felt had wracked his entire body. Sweat dripped into his eyes from his brow, and David wiped it with his left forearm. He looked at the cut again. It was clean and red, the edges of the parted skin livid, but it was far from being a mortal wound. The pain had dulled to a throbbing ache which radiated up through his wrist. He clenched his hand to dull it further, and dark-red drops of blood squeezed out between his fingers and dripped on to the ground.

David had some tissue in his pocket, so he wiped the blood vigorously with it and then pressed the tissue against the cut to stop the bleeding. He got to his feet, his legs wobbling slightly, and he steeled himself to look at the tree trunk.

At the spot where he'd touched it was a thorn. He'd obviously placed his hand on this without noticing, and the spike had cut the palm of his hand. He could see his blood on the bark. He was almost relieved by the smallness of the thorn, and he rationalized that perhaps it had been the sudden shock and surprise that had made him feel so much pain.

His blood was already drying into the skin of the tree. In fact, it looked as if it was being sucked into it right in front of his eyes.

David rubbed a hand across his eyes to clear his vision, but yes, there it was, a ruby-red droplet of his blood being drawn right into the tree like water soaking into a tissue. He shivered, and tried to move.

David wanted to run.

'*Shhhhh,*' said the breeze. '*Look.*'

David felt calmed by the voice. *Is it a voice?* he thought. *Am I imagining it?*

The spot where his blood had been absorbed started to swell ever so slightly. It was as if the tree bark had suddenly become soft and pliable, more skin than bark. David watched in horrified fascination as the small lump started to pulse. Up and down it went, up and down, like a vein throbbing in a neck. It was oval-shaped, and something about that shape was terribly familiar.

Then the oval shape suddenly stopped pulsing.

The oval shape opened . . .

. . . and David found himself staring at an amber eye.

For one terrifying moment he couldn't take in what he was seeing.

The eye glared at him, then blinked, then its gaze started to dart left and right as if panicked by its predicament.

David stumbled backwards and fell against one of the roots of the tree. The eye fixed its manic glare on him again. David was frozen in horror as he watched what happened next.

The eye blinked rapidly, dozens, hundreds of times in quick succession. The dark leathery bark of the tree surrounding the eye pulsed and roiled and stretched. David gave a low moan of terror.

Look, said the voice. *Look*.

The skin of the tree seemed to redouble its efforts. It twisted and convulsed, and now David could see a discernible shape forming. It had limbs, it had a head. A sharp protuberance looked like a nose. Another eye blinked open, and David's heart started to *pound pound pound* against his ribcage.

The figure in the tree started to separate itself from the trunk. There were splintering sounds – *spok*, *pok*, *thuk* – as the being within began to free itself. Wood splintered as the figure buried in the tree started to wrench itself out like something that had been trapped in mud, and then with a shrill scream the thing was free.

'*Shhhhh,*' said the breeze.

But David was no longer listening. He turned and ran.

CHAPTER
6

The days passed. The Cresswells unpacked all their boxes. Everyone forgot about the incident with the books. They had other things on their minds.

David said nothing about his experience in the forest. He fobbed Penny and his father off with something about cutting the palm of his hand on a splinter on the banister. It gave him an excuse to vent about the house, and as his father listened patiently Penny knew David was lying, particularly when she saw the panicked way he ranted. Their father didn't press David on the subject. Like so many other problems he'd dealt with since their mum had died, he seemed to give up on the matter almost straight away.

The days passed, and they went about rebuilding

their lives.

In the attic Pog waited and watched.

And in the forest something moved through the dark.

PART 2

What Was Promised

CHAPTER 7

The sound was soft in the dark. Low and murmurous in the night it came, but Pog heard it, even as he slept.

He rolled over, immediately awake, and sprang up on to his feet. He stood in the attic, trembling in anticipation as he sniffed the air and strained his ears.

'What's to do now, Pog?' he whispered.

That smell. He knew that smell. Dry, mustardy.

Pog snarled and bared his teeth. 'No,' he growled.

He grabbed his sword and staff and climbed up into the rafters and out through the hole in the roof. He slid down the old rusty drainpipe, and landed with a soft thump on the ground.

He sniffed again and nodded. There was a sound too, moist and screechy. A low rumble started to build in Pog's throat. He clasped the hilt of his sword and headed towards the source of the sound. He passed an open window. The scent trail came from inside the window, and down along the wall. 'Come through the Necessary they have,' he said, berating himself for not realizing sooner. He rounded the corner of the house, and there they were.

He didn't need the light of the moon to see them. Three of them. They weren't fully grown adults, and consequently not as vicious, but they were as big as fists, eight-legged tawny creatures with almost-human faces, chittering to each other.

'Greebeldies!' Pog hissed.

They all turned sharply in his direction, their screeching like nails on a blackboard. Pog drew his sword and staff and crouched low. 'Come now, face Pog,' he snarled.

The three greebeldies charged him.

Pog had a sack on his person for such emergencies. He unfurled it from inside his jacket with one hand, and with his other he flicked his staff, hitting one of his assailants. It gave a startled squeak and fell to the ground, stunned. Pog scooped it up and threw it in his sack, but the other two had leapt on his back and were now gnashing their teeth.

Pog didn't think twice. He ran backwards into the wall and felt a mixture of satisfaction and guilt when he heard the collective 'Oof' they gave. He had twirled around and grabbed them before they hit the ground. He flung them into his sack and drew the drawstring tight. He took a moment to catch his breath. There was a twitch from the sack, and Pog poked it gently with the end of his staff.

'Told youse before. No coming through. Stay on your side. But do youse listen? No, you—'

Rustling from above. Pog looked up to see another greebeldy crawling up through the ivy towards a window.

Pog slung the sack over his shoulder and then launched himself at the wall. He scrambled up, but the creature was already on the windowsill. Pog accelerated. He was just centimetres away. He grabbed for one of its legs, but missed. The thing tumbled in through the window, and Pog sprang the last few centimetres, landed on the sill and then rolled into the room, somersaulting and landing with a soft thud on the floorboards.

The greebeldy had found what it was looking for. It was already on the bed, and it was looming over the sleeping form of the girl. Pog froze for a moment as he watched the greebeldy open its mouth in a horrible grin. It slowly reached over the girl with two of its legs, the pincers on each end opening and closing in excited anticipation. A globule of drool dripped from the corner of its mouth and on to the sheet. The greebeldy quivered with delight as its pincer closed around its target.

Pog leapt.

He took the greebeldy full in the face with his staff. The greebeldy spun through the air. Pog landed on the ground, caught it in mid-air, gave it a swift punch to silence it, and then dropped the dazed greebeldy into his sack. All of this was accomplished with the minimum of noise and movement.

The object the greebeldy had snatched fluttered to the ground. Pog picked it up.

It was one of the pictures of the girl and her family. Pog's whole body suddenly trembled with rage. He snarled at the sack.

'Memories. You was sucking memories again. Memories that ain't yours!'

Pog looked at the picture again. There was a faint gossamer flickering of light around it, a sure sign that the greebeldy had already been feeding on the picture. Greebeldies liked memories. They knew that everything tall folk touched was infused with them, and there was nothing more delicious to greebeldies than memories. They gorged themselves on them, fattened on them. They particularly liked the most powerful memories, those filled with pain. The more important the object, the more powerful and nourishing these painful memories were.

Pog couldn't help himself. He gave the sack a quick thump with his stick, enjoying the muffled squeaks.

He crept towards the bed, the picture in his paw. The girl's eyes were closed, but she was frowning. Pog slowly slid the picture on to the bed and under her hand. The girl's face relaxed slightly. Pog tilted his head. He wondered why holding the picture brought her such comfort, even as she slept. Only something soaked in pain could attract so many greebeldies at once. Surely there was no comfort in that. What did it all mean?

The girl twitched and started to turn. Pog ducked down under the bed with his sack. He listened to her breathing and waited until it became regular again. He crept out and threw one wary eye in the girl's direction, but her face was turned away towards the door.

Pog crawled out from under the bed and headed

for the window. With one last curious look at the girl, he hoisted the sack over his back and clambered down the wall.

Thoughts fizzed around inside his head as Pog made his way out of the gate and away from the house.

Is the Necessary holding?

''Course it is,' he said defiantly, as he reached his destination inside the forest.

But there seemed to be more creatures coming through than usual. Sometimes months would have passed before Pog would have encountered anything, but recently the number seemed to be increasing. The last time Pog had seen such a surge was when the older tall ones had lived in the house. It had started just before they moved in, as if the creatures on the other side of the Necessary could sense their coming. It had subsided when they left.

Always be paying attention, Pog.

Pog licked his lips and shook his head. No, there were many greebeldies this time, but it meant nothing. All these things passing through was just a freak occurrence. The Necessary was holding. It would always hold, he told himself.

And yet these tall ones had something different about them. It was as if they carried something.

Something that weighed them down, something the greebeldies and their like could smell.

Pog could feel a prickling along his spine.

He put the sack on the ground and poked the wriggling mass with his staff. 'Youse listen now. Pog knows youse came through the gaps, but Pog is merciful. Pog could throw you through the Necessary back where youse belong, and youse could get eaten by all sorts and whatnots because youse are young and small, but Pog will let youse loose so long's as youse stay away from the house.'

The wriggling slowed. Pog tapped the sack with his stick.

'Does we have an understanding?'

The wriggling stopped completely.

Pog nodded. 'Good so.'

He bent down and untied the sack. The greebeldies sped off into the forest, the leader taking one last chance to turn its head and shriek something at Pog before it darted off into the night.

'Pog thinks you smell worse!' Pog shouted.

He tried to forget all about things coming through the Necessary, so instead he thought about the girl and her picture, how her hair looked the same as the woman's. Something about their faces niggled him, but Pog couldn't lay a finger on it.

There was also something about the picture that gave him a heavy feeling in his chest.

A family together. Happy and smiling.

Pog thought about Grandfa. He stood for a moment looking out into the night, and a sudden feeling of terrible loneliness washed over him.

CHAPTER 8

'We have a rat.'

Penny looked at her surroundings. The interior of the shed was the brownest thing she'd ever seen. It was filled with bits of old wood, rusted pots and pans, and decaying cardboard boxes. She turned to David.

'You brought me out to the shed to tell me that?' she said.

David just looked at her. His brow knotted as he fixed her with a look of belligerent determination. It was a look that never seemed to waver. His eyes were dark and tinged with fury.

Penny gestured at the interior of the shed. 'It's just that if there's a rat, this is a pretty good place for it to hide in.'

David shook his head vigorously. He looked so

terribly earnest, like a child half his age fixated on a new toy. Penny found it almost comical, but also, if she was being honest with herself, just a little sad.

'There was something outside my room the other night.' David started to dig through some of the rubbish on the shelf behind him.

Penny shook her head. 'I didn't hear anything,' she said.

David just grunted as he threw bits and pieces aside to get to what he needed. Eventually he turned around to display a large rat trap between his thumb and forefinger while gesturing at the pile of them which he'd uncovered.

'We're going to catch it with these,' he said.

'We?'

David nodded. Penny noticed the dark circles under his eyes, and she felt a sudden ache of pity. David started to warm to his topic.

'It was dark, but I definitely saw something. I think it might be hiding in the attic, or in the walls. You must have heard it?'

Penny shook her head.

David scowled and looked at the floor as if he was now only talking to himself. 'Doesn't matter, I've heard it a few times. I have good hearing. Just like—'

Just like Mum, thought Penny.

David's eyes flitted to her for a moment, and then away back to the floor. He started biting his upper lip.

'We should tell Dad,' she said.

'No!' said David. The vehemence of his response surprised her.

'Why not?'

David sneered. 'Because he'll start taking the rat's side and he'll be talking about' – David made air quotes – '*preserving the environment and respecting the ecosystem.*'

'He'll be useless in other words,' Penny sighed.

'Well, yeah.'

Penny mulled it over. She wasn't particularly happy with the idea that a large rodent might be roaming the house. That said, she wasn't entirely sure that David was right. He could well be imagining things. It was a new house after all, and getting used to strange new noises was part of moving in. She looked at her brother again and saw how pale and drawn his face looked. He'd been acting strange lately. Sometimes he was withdrawn, and his eyes had a guarded look about them. At other times he seemed incredibly agitated, and he would scratch the palm of his hand, his eyes darting every which way, as if he was expecting something to leap out at him at any moment.

Penny supposed it was partly to do with losing Mum. The move couldn't have helped him either.

'All right then,' she said.

Immediately David's eyes lit up, and the colour seemed to flow back into his cheeks. Penny felt relieved at his reaction.

'So what do we do?' she asked.

'We lay traps, but in places and at times where and when we know Dad won't see them.'

Penny nodded, to show how reasonable she thought the idea was. 'And where do we start?'

David gave a sly grin. 'We start with the attic.'

David had planned everything down to a T. Dad had gone to the shops. The house was eight miles from the village, and David knew he would be at least half an hour. He and Penny dragged an old dirty ladder from the shed and hauled it up the stairs. It was just as well their dad was out. The *kathump-kathump* of the ladder on each step echoed through the house. David blamed Penny for the sound. Penny blamed David. But all recriminations were forgotten when they raised the ladder and pushed it against the attic door.

Penny felt a strange tickling excitement as she looked up at the narrow triangle of shadow that now opened up between the lip of the door and the darkness beyond. It was silly, she thought. They were only going looking for a rat, and while the thought of it made her feel slightly queasy, she was strangely thrilled to be engaged in this task.

They shoved the ladder this way and that, both swaying like sailors on a wind-whipped deck, until finally the ladder hooks found purchase against the lip of the attic opening.

David was first up, a rat trap in each hand banging against the sides of the ladder. When he got to the top he shoved the door aside. There was a groaning scrape as it rubbed against the edge, and Penny saw him wipe a hand on the side of his jeans. He looked down at her and curled his lip. 'Careful, it's filthy.'

She watched him disappear into the attic, and then she started her own ascent. She could smell the air in the attic just before she poked her head in. There was a hot tang to it that travelled to the back of her throat.

David was standing a few metres in front of her, shining a torch at the roof. He was holding his beloved rat traps in his left hand as he cocked his head at an angle. Penny gave him a moment before she spoke:

'Do you think—'

'Shhh!'

Penny listened to the silence.

'I thought I heard something,' David hissed.

'I don't hear anything,' said Penny.

David turned to look at her, his brow furrowed, a look of fierce concentration on his face. 'We have to look for poo,' he said.

Penny slapped a hand to her mouth, and she almost choked with laughter. She had no idea what was so funny. Maybe it was the look on David's face – so serious, as if he was on the most secret, most dangerous mission ever.

David was not impressed with her reaction: 'It's what you have to do. You look for rat droppings.'

Penny kept her hand clamped to her mouth and bent over with her other hand raised. 'Give me a minute,' she said in a strangled voice.

David shook his head and sighed. 'Rat droppings are evidence that a rat is about. And puddles of wee.'

'Wee?'

'Yes, wee,' said an exasperated David.

'Are we looking for wee too?' Penny snorted.

'Yes. Shut up.'

David glared at her. Penny composed herself. She breathed out, then breathed the air back in again and was immediately sorry.

She flapped a hand in front of her mouth and made a little 'gah' sound. 'Actually, can we stop talking about wee and poo?'

'Just look, would you?' David sighed again.

Penny turned to look behind her. The attic stretched the length of the house. It was a huge dark space, buttressed with old, crumbly-looking rafters. It went so far back that the wall furthest away from them disappeared into the gloom. There were patches in the arched ceiling where light seeped through some gauzy material. There were some small puddles of water on the floor, but they were positioned right under the patches.

'Just rainwater,' said David, looking at one of the puddles.

'Do you want to taste it, to be sure?' asked Penny.

David looked horrified.

Penny giggled. 'Lighten up.'

She took another look around her. The overall sensation she felt was of an overbearing darkness. She couldn't help but think of the attic in their old house which had doubled as a study. It was where her mother drew her sketches. The walls had been made from painted wood that was creamy and bright. The whole room was a womb of light, and Penny remembered her mother lifting her up and letting her look through the attic window as the sun set over the city. She remembered her mother's arms around her, and the way the sun spilt golden across the rooftops, bathing everything in honeyed warmth. On bright days the window was a fierce rectangle of blue, and she felt she could breathe that blue right into her. It made her feel strong. It seemed to her the colour and light of that room promised hope and happiness.

David turned and swept the torchlight in a full circle. For a moment a grey shape was illuminated in the dark.

'Look,' said Penny. She walked towards the shape, and David turned his light back on it.

It was an old rocking horse. One of its hind legs was missing, and one of the eye sockets was empty, web-like fractures radiating from its circumference.

Penny touched the horse's neck as if shushing an actual live animal.

'Over here!' said David.

He had illuminated a pile of old rags and wood in a corner. There was what looked like a ragged blanket and a makeshift pillow in the centre of the mess, almost as if someone had arranged it to sleep in.

'It's like someone's den,' said David.

Penny looked back at the rocking horse. 'A family must have lived here a long time ago.'

'You reckon some Victorian kids did that?' David waved his torch at the pile, and wrinkled his nose in disgust. 'What's that?' he added, almost nudging Penny aside to bend down so he could have a closer look at something on the floor. He picked something up. It was a short black wooden stick with designs carved into it. 'Some kind of stick,' he said.

'Let me see,' said Penny.

He handed it to her. It was surprisingly warm.

David put his hand out and smiled. 'Keepsies. I found it.'

Penny handed it back to him and they went back to shining their torches around the floor.

'Any poo?' asked Penny.

'No poo,' said David.

'Don't sound so disappointed.'

They continued to scan the floor. Penny did her own tour, finding clumps of old newspapers which were covered in dirt and had mouldered together to make great big fungal lumps. She found a porcelain doll's head, a yellowed doily, some stained brass candlesticks. Everything was covered in dust and mould.

She leant against a wall without thinking. Immediately she felt something filthy against the palm of her hand and recoiled. 'Euugh!' she said.

'What is it?' said David, spinning round with the torch.

Penny held up the palm of her hand for him to see, and wiped away the remains of the old decayed cobweb, trying to ignore the tiny, many-legged, desiccated spider corpses it contained.

She and David exchanged a look of understanding, and without a second's thought both spoke the exact same word at the exact same time:

'Greebeldies!'

A 'greebeldy' was their mum's word for anything with six legs or more that was considered vile and disgusting. It was a word for something that came out of the dark with terrible intent. Their mum used to make up bedtime stories about greebeldies, and David and Penny would shriek with delight and terror at her tales, and their mum would smile. As they grew older, 'greebeldy' became a general family word for all the bad things in life.

David sniggered first, and Penny started sniggering along with him. Before they knew it they were both laughing with tears streaming out of their eyes.

'Greebeldies,' Penny squealed, and this just seemed to make them both laugh even harder. Penny had no idea why they were laughing, and she had a sudden vision of her mother shrieking in the bathroom one day as she did a little dance over a spider which she'd spotted in the bath.

David was bent double now, and the torchlight was wobbling. He wiped his nose and snorted. Penny felt light-headed, and she could feel the laughter subsiding. She wiped the corner of her eyes, and she said 'greebeldies' once more, and this just set them both off all over again.

After a couple more minutes of sobbing laughter, Penny could feel herself return to normal. The lightness started to fade, and the heaviness returned. It was the first time she'd felt that way since their mum had died, and that realization made the sensation of great weight she now felt even more constricting. She could feel it settle over her chest and press down on her shoulders, and now more than anything she just wanted that sensation of happiness and lightness to return.

'We should put these traps down anyway,' said David, all business again.

'OK,' Penny agreed, wiping a hand across her nose.

She watched him place both traps at separate walls. He took a hunk of cheese from his pocket and dug into it with his fingers, taking chunks out of it and placing them on each trap. He set the traps. Penny could feel herself tensing as he pulled the mechanisms back. They were large traps and she was scared they'd take off the top of a finger if not handled properly. She let out a great sigh of relief when the last one was set.

David dusted the palms of his hands on his thighs and looked at his handiwork. 'Let's see it escape *those*,' he said.

He and Penny started towards the ladder. Penny went first, looking above her at the stick poking out of David's back pocket. He put the attic door back in place, and they both took hold of the ladder and headed down the stairs and back out towards the shed. David took the front of the ladder and Penny took the rear. As they walked, Penny found she couldn't take her eyes off the stick.

They deposited the ladder back in the shed, and David came out and stood with his hands on his hips, looking very pleased with himself: 'We'll set the rest of them when Dad's asleep.'

Penny wasn't really listening to him. She was still pondering something. 'Let me see that again,' she said, pointing at the stick.

David handed it to her.

Penny turned the stick over in her hands, her brow furrowing in concentration. 'That's odd,' she said.

'What's odd?' said David.

'It's old,' said Penny.

'So?' said David. 'We know it's old.'

She held it up for him to see. 'Yes, but everything up there was filthy. If this is so old, then why is it so clean?'

CHAPTER 9

Pog slid himself from the rafter where he'd been hiding and swung down on his rope.

His heart was hammering as he scampered across the floor.

Gone. They'd taken it. Grandfa's staff was gone.

Pog rubbed his face in agitation and cursed himself. He hadn't been paying attention and the two small tall ones had been up and into the attic before he'd known it. He'd been dozing and savouring a dream that was green and blue and soft. It was a lovely dream, a reminder of home, and it had distracted him. He'd smelt the two children before he'd heard them, and by then it was almost too late.

Stupid Pog. Silly Pog.

He stamped his two feet in anger. Pog was cross, cross with the two small ones, but most of all he was cross with himself.

What's to do now, Pog?

Pog stood up and raised his chin and whispered into the dark.

'Pog gets it back. That's what's to do now.'

CHAPTER 10

It was around three in the morning when Penny felt a hand on her shoulder. She turned around to see David looking down at her.

'Come quick,' he said.

Penny stumbled out to the landing to find him pointing at something.

'Two of them went off,' he hissed. '*Two* of them.'

Penny looked at the two traps and rubbed her eyes. Both had been set off. Both lay at awkward angles.

And both of them were empty.

David stood there pointing at them, his teeth bared. He looked like he was about to burst into tears.

'And it took the cheese!'

'Shhh,' Penny said. 'You'll wake Dad.' Although

she didn't really think that their dad would wake (he was a heavy sleeper), she just wanted to calm David down. He'd grabbed fistfuls of his own hair and was staring in disbelief, his elbows sticking out and away from his head.

His eyes suddenly flashed to the left and he lowered his arms as if he'd just realized something.

'They say they're intelligent,' he said, more to himself than Penny.

'Who says?' asked Penny.

'Scientists. They say rats are intelligent. I saw it on the telly. They can get out of mazes and things, and they can do simple puzzles.' He narrowed his eyes and gave one of those dark malicious grins of his. 'This one's just really intelligent.' David tapped the side of this head. 'Which means we have to be smarter.'

'Right,' said Penny, with as much interest as she could muster, considering the late hour.

David frowned. 'Or was that parrots or chimpanzees that could do puzzles?'

'David.'

'What?'

'Go to bed.' When he didn't move she said, 'We'll try the traps again tomorrow night, I promise.'

David blinked, finally seeming a little less crazed

and a little more tired and rational-looking. He relented and headed into his bedroom. Watching him close his bedroom door made Penny feel hugely relieved for some reason she couldn't place. She turned away and was walking across the landing when she felt something lumpy beneath her slipper. She moved her foot and bent down to pick up a small piece of cheese. She rolled it between thumb and forefinger as she looked at it, then she looked left and right, and for some reason something made her look up.

The attic door was directly above her. In the gloom there was a gap where one edge of it looked slightly gnawed. She wasn't sure, but something about that small sliver of darkness made her wary. She looked around. It felt like she was being watched, and she could feel a shiver worm its way up the centre of her back and across her shoulders. Stubbornly she shook it off.

'Stupid,' she said to herself. 'Stupid.'

Still admonishing herself she went back into her bedroom.

CHAPTER 11

Penny's eyes were sticky from not having had enough sleep the previous night. She rubbed them, but she found she was looking through a grey fog as David sat across the kitchen table from her, so she didn't entirely trust what she was seeing. What he seemed to be doing was glaring at her as he spooned his porridge into his mouth.

'Where is it?' David said.

Penny rubbed her eyes again and blinked a few times in an attempt to focus on him. 'Where's what?'

David looked disgusted with her response. He was just about to jab his spoon in Penny's direction when their dad entered.

'Morning,' he said, padding into the kitchen in his slippers. He went to the cupboard, grabbed a cereal box and started to pour it into a bowl.

Penny and David mumbled their hellos as Dad poured milk on his cereal. David took advantage of the fact that he had his back turned to both of them and he started to lean over the table towards Penny. He raised his eyebrows.

'What?' said Penny.

'You know what,' David hissed.

Dad passed David on his way out the door, and he absent-mindedly ruffled his hair. He was completely oblivious to the tension building in the room. David didn't even notice the hair ruffling; he just kept glaring at Penny, who was giving as good as she got in the glaring department.

'I don't know what you're talking about.'

'Yes you do.'

'No I don't, that's why I said I don't know what you're talking about.'

David sighed and leant back. 'The stick.'

'What about it?'

David propped himself forward again. 'You took it.'

Penny was completely bemused. 'No I didn't.'

For the first time David looked unsure of himself. 'Well, it's gone.'

'I didn't take it. Anyway, why would I take it?'

'I don't know.' David shrugged. 'Maybe . . .' He

didn't seem to know how to finish his train of thought.

'Where did you have it?' asked Penny.

'Under my pillow.'

Penny's eyes narrowed. 'Are you sure you just didn't mislay it?'

David folded his arms and rolled his eyes. 'Yes.'

'Well, it wasn't me who took it.'

Penny saw the doubt creep into his eyes, then the sudden look of panic and rage. He jumped up from his chair. 'You took it, Pen. Just admit it!' He headed for the door.

'Where are you going?' Penny said.

'For a walk!' David shouted, storming out of the kitchen.

In his study, Dad had his easel up and his workstool in front of it. He'd also positioned his desk by the window. There were boxes and sheets of paper all over the floor. When Penny entered the room he was rubbing his hands nervously and he cocked his head towards the easel.

'What do you think?'

Penny looked at it. The sheet which was held in place on the easel had lots of lines on it with some measurements and arrows. It looked complicated, but typically of her dad's work, it also somehow looked like he'd thrown it together casually.

'Looks good, Dad. What is it?'

He grinned. 'My plans for the house,' he said.

He started to tell her what everything represented, and he did that thing he did when he got excited talking about a project, and he began to form shapes in the air with his hands. Penny nodded and smiled, but truth be told she couldn't really understand exactly what he was trying to describe. There was lots of talk about 'bringing the outside in' and 'making it arboreal to fit in with its woodland surroundings' and 'open-plan, but warm and inviting'.

'Sounds great, Dad,' smiled Penny.

'Thanks,' her dad replied, standing there wringing his hands as if waiting for something from her, another compliment perhaps, or a question. Penny wasn't sure what. He was still smiling, but Penny found his eyes hard to look at. They were the eyes of someone lost and a little bit desperate, and looking at them made her feel slightly embarrassed for him.

'Your mum would have liked it, I think,' he said, clearing his throat and shoving his glasses further up his nose.

Penny clenched her fists. 'Dad, I—'

'Yeah, I think so,' he continued, looking around the room in an attempt to avoid her eyes. 'Not so sure what your great-grandma Rose would have thought of my messing about with her ancestral home though.' He gave a nervous chuckle, and there was that hopeful desperate look again. His face suddenly slackened. 'We were planning on moving here and doing it up, before . . .'

We. Penny felt a stinging at the corner of her eyes.

'She loved coming here when she was young,' Dad said quietly. 'She used to tell me that she felt really at home here. That she felt at peace. This was a really happy place for her. The stories she used to tell.' He smiled nervously. 'Maybe we could all find some peace here like your mum did, maybe we could . . .'

He trailed off and shook his head, as if admonishing himself for saying something stupid. Penny felt the urge to move towards him, but it was as if her feet were stuck in mud.

Her dad started to move hesitantly towards the desk, casting occasional apologetic glances her way, and Penny felt the sudden return of that irritation she'd recently started to feel in his presence, but she kept smiling.

He started to absently flick through some of the

pages on his desk, pursing his lips and furrowing his brow in pretend concentration. Penny couldn't shake the feeling that he was like a child trying to be an adult.

'So, how are you then?' he asked without looking at her.

'Me?'

'Yes. How are you then, Pen? *Then Pen*. That's nearly a poem,' he said, giving a weak chuckle.

'Fine. Yes. Fine,' said Penny, clearing her throat because it seemed to be hard to get the words out.

Her dad looked at her. 'Fine? That's good, that's good. I'm glad.' They both stood there just looking at each other. Her dad's face twitched. 'Pen?'

'What, Dad?' She sounded a little irritated, didn't she? She cursed herself. She hadn't meant to sound like that.

'I was wondering . . . I was thinking . . . I mean, how are you and David really?'

Penny felt a sudden moment of panic. It must have showed on her face because her dad's voice started to quicken:

'I mean, what I'm saying is, are you both happy to be here in this house?'

For a moment Penny didn't know what to say. Her father's eyes searched her face, and she found herself blurting something out, anything just to fill up the awkward silence.

'Yes, absolutely. It's brilliant here. I can't speak for David but he really likes it too.'

Stupid, she thought to herself. *How stupid was that? I can't speak for David, but I'll speak for him anyway.* That made no sense.

Her dad nodded. 'Good, that's good, because I want this to be a new start for us. So that we can push on.' He made a 'push on' gesture with his arm and fist which both he and Penny knew instantly looked slightly ridiculous.

'Right,' said Penny. 'I should go,' she said.

'Right,' said her dad.

'What about you, Dad? How are you?'

For a moment he looked slightly stunned by the question. His mouth opened and he couldn't seem to say anything, but eventually he managed to paste on that all-too-familiar fake smile again.

'Fine,' he said, 'absolutely fine.'

CHAPTER 12

David was further into the forest than he'd realized. He'd left the path without knowing it and was now well in among the trees. The wind was starting to rise, and it was making a low 'whooming' sound through the branches.

He squinted into the dark heart of the forest.

Part of him wanted to see something. Part of him was afraid. And yet he could feel that magnetic pull compelling him forward. His palm where he'd cut himself was starting to itch and he scratched it.

Despite his reluctance, he started to walk forward. He didn't want to, and yet he felt as if he couldn't resist. It was as if his legs were no longer his own, and his arms, which now felt like lead, were hanging by his sides. *Where am I going?*

You know exactly where you're going, said a sly inner voice.

That eye again. David could see a flash of amber, and he could sense its rage and panic.

'No!' he shouted, and he wrenched himself back around, his arms flapping by his sides like something from a bad zombie movie.

Keep walking away, just keep walking, he told himself.

The pressure pushing him backwards was immense. It was like walking through the waves at the edge of a seashore when the tide suddenly recedes and you can feel the suck of the water as it tries to pull you out. He clenched his teeth and pushed on.

Eventually he reached the road again and the pressure seemed to ease. He was panting and sweating, and he took a moment to look back at the forest.

He turned back around and almost walked straight on to the corpse of a bird. David pulled up with a start, and his heart hammered in his chest.

The bird was just lying there, eyes glazed, its neck broken. There was dried blood on its brown wings. There was another lying just a few metres from it. It too had had its neck broken. David looked around him.

'What's going on?' he pleaded.

The wind was low and murmurous. The forest wasn't telling.

CHAPTER 13

P enny sat on the edge of her bed. She could feel the sobs coming. The world was already fracturing, crystalline and jagged as the tears filled her eyes.

After the feeling passed, she stood up and wiped her eyes and face with some tissue. *I have to keep moving*, she thought. If you kept moving it meant you could keep one step ahead of the thing that followed you: the dark ravenous thing that wanted to devour you. She needed to occupy her mind with something else.

The stick, that was it. She'd look for the stick.

She started in David's room, looking under the bed, in his wardrobe, behind his chest of drawers. She found nothing but dust bunnies. She checked the landing, the stairs and the hallway. She passed by her father's study and was relieved to see the door was shut. She tiptoed past it and headed into the depths of the house.

Since arriving, Penny hadn't shown any interest in exploring the house. Once upon a time she might have jumped at the chance, but not now. Lately she'd lost interest in a lot of things that she used to enjoy.

She felt the hollowness rise within her again, and she tried to dampen it down by concentrating on the task at hand. As she walked down the hallway that led to the rear of the house, she found herself blinking. It was as if the light was flickering; gloomy one moment, bright the next, until finally it seemed to settle into a dull-brown luminescence. The air also seemed to change, light and airy one moment, heavy and damp the next. Penny decided it was all just another symptom of her not getting enough sleep.

She passed the cellar door, then suddenly stopped. Her father had already warned both her and David not to go near it. He said that subsidence was a big problem, and that the cellar could be dangerous. Penny reckoned there was no way the stick might be in there, but she felt drawn to the door. It was old and splintered, unvarnished and almost furry-looking. Someone had daubed a dull-blue squiggle across the bottom, probably as part of an attempted paint job that had gone unfinished. The squiggle was faded with age.

Penny looked at the squiggle and she felt a dull throbbing in the centre of her forehead, and she pinched the bridge of her nose. She turned her face away and the throbbing sensation vanished. She turned to look at the squiggle again, and the throbbing returned, as if a switch had been flicked.

That's weird, she thought.

She tried looking away and back again. Each time the result was the same.

'That's really weird,' she whispered.

Penny clasped the brass knob and turned it, but the door held fast. Penny tried to remember where she had seen some old skeleton keys when they'd first arrived. It came to her immediately, and she scurried back to the cubbyhole under the stairs. She squeezed into the tight musty space and she spotted the keys on a hook at head height. She snatched them and headed back to the cellar door.

The first seven of the keys were useless. Some were too small, some too large. It was with key number eight that she finally had a bit of luck. It slotted in perfectly, and there was the satisfying clunk as tumblers turned. Penny smiled as she turned the doorknob.

And yet the door still stubbornly refused to open.

Penny frowned. She turned the key again, locked the door, then unlocked it. She turned the knob and pushed the door. Nothing happened.

She examined the door jamb, wondering if somehow it been sealed shut. She couldn't see anything, and when she put her fingertips to the edges she could feel a cool draught.

She tried the key a few more times before eventually giving up. She looked at the door surround and frowned. There were irregular cracks radiating outward from the edge of the door and along the wall. She made a note to mention it to her father. It was probably something to do with the subsidence. She made her way back to the cubbyhole, completely perplexed by what had happened, and was just putting the keys back when she heard the front door open.

She stepped out of the cubbyhole and was surprised to see that David was standing in the hallway, a little out of breath and sweating. His fringe was standing up in spikes.

'Hi,' she said.

'Hi,' he panted in response.

'Were you out running or something?'

David rolled his eyes at her. It was only a small gesture, but it was annoying enough for Penny to decide against telling him about the cellar. While she was thinking, David had started to scratch his hand.

'Is it itchy?' she said.

'What?' David replied, looking slightly irritated.

'Your hand,' Penny said. 'You keep scratching it. Is it itchy?'

'I told you, I caught it on a splinter, that's all,' he snapped.

Penny noticed the droplets of sweat on his forehead. His eyes were large and wide, as if he was on the verge of panic. She put the palm of her right hand to his forehead, and David flinched.

'What are you doing?'

'Checking your temperature,' said Penny.

David sneered. 'Who do you think you are – Mum?'

Penny felt a quick sharp shock that was gone before she could even fully register it. She blinked, and David blinked rapidly in response, and took half a step backwards. He looked guilty for a moment, then angry.

No, Penny thought. *I don't think I'm Mum. Although everybody says I look like her and I hate it when they say that. I hate it.*

'You just look like you might have a fever, that's all,' she snapped.

'Well, I don't,' David snapped back.

'Fine,' said Penny.

'Fine,' said David, jamming his hands in his pockets and giving her a surly sideways glance. He left her in the hall and pounded up the stairs. Penny watched him go.

I'm not like Mum, she thought to herself. *Mum would be all worried about you and your fever. Burn up. See if I care.*

CHAPTER 14

Night found Pog back downstairs. He kept a tight hold of his staff as he went about his duties. He wasn't about to lose it a second time.

First he went to the sitting room. He stood at the fireplace looking up at the bronze object on the mantelpiece, wondering to himself what it might be. It contained something important, Pog guessed that much. But what exactly? It was too small to contain anything as important as the Necessary. Pog scratched his forehead and frowned. He shook his head. Perhaps it was best to leave the tall ones to their secrets.

The tall ones were abed. They'd been there for hours now. He could feel them breathing. It was like whispers by his ear, soft and low and reassuring.

The father was deep and away elsewhere as always, and the girl was also in a deep slumber, but occasionally Pog's ears would twitch as he caught the boy whimpering. Sometimes there were words, but these were muffled. Pog wasn't too worried. As long as he didn't hear a tell-tale gasp as they woke, or the creak of a floorboard, he knew he was OK.

After he was finished in the sitting room he headed towards the cellar door. Pog was delighted to see Mouse waiting for him in the hallway, and he followed Pog to the door.

Pog laid his palm on the door, and then leant his face against it. He closed his eyes and nodded in satisfaction, and then turned to Mouse.

'So you see, Mouse, this is the way it be since the old times and the promise was made between each Lumpkin what came before. Pog does his duty like Grandfa and his father before him. Pog keeps the promise. Pog guards the Necessary like what Grandfa did, to ensure nothing passes through. Pog holds fast and doesn't waver. The Necessary holds so long as Pog is Guardian.'

Mouse was scampering around sniffing at skirting boards. He didn't seem too bothered either way about what Pog was saying, but Pog didn't mind. He was just glad of the company.

Pog smiled to himself when he thought of all the others who had come before, all of those who had kept the promise. He was proud to be counted among their number – although he wouldn't admit that to Mouse. Being boastful and prideful was not the way of the First Folk. Being courageous but modest was the best way of things. Being—

He stiffened. His ears twitched, and he sniffed the air. 'What's that, Mouse?' he whispered.

Pog headed straight for the kitchen. The air was clearer in there. Once inside he hopped up on to the kitchen sink. Mouse scuttled in behind him.

Pog turned towards the kitchen window. There was only blackness outside, but Pog knew that was never the full story with the night.

There's always something in the dark, Grandfa said.

He crouched at the edge of the sink and was dead still, all muscles tensed, only a gentle quivering through his body revealing that he was in fact alive and not a tiny statue.

Pog listened again.

Pog sniffed the air.

There was something on the wind.

It couldn't be, Pog thought. Nothing could have passed through the Necessary and out into the world without him knowing.

He leant forward and squinted into the dark. He didn't move for a full five minutes, and as he sniffed, and as he listened, his hackles became raised and his nose and mouth curled in a silent snarl.

'Something's afoot, Mouse,' he said.

Mouse didn't reply. There wasn't even the tiny tremble of a mouse whisker on the kitchen air.

Pog turned to look at Mouse, but Mouse was gone. Pog had been so busy concentrating on what might be outside he hadn't noticed Mouse leave the kitchen.

And then Pog heard the snap of steel.

He heard the tiny shriek in the distance.

'Mouse!' Pog roared.

He sprang across the kitchen and out the door.

CHAPTER 15

Penny was back home in London. She was in the garden. The sun was beating down, and the lawn was a fiery lime green.

She held her head up and felt the warmth on her face. The heat of the sunlight was just a smidgen away from being too stifling.

That was when she heard the voice calling her name.

'Mum?' she said, her lips moving thickly.

She went into the house, the kitchen first, calling for her mother. There was no sign of her. She went into the sitting room next and that too was empty. She ran into the hallway. As she searched she became aware that the whole house was empty, and the truth finally hit her that she was the only person inside. She looked outside through the glass beside the hallway door, and the street was warm and bathed in sunlight, and it too was empty and silent. For some reason the warmth and brightness of the day made it all the more unnerving.

She started to panic. The sensation of being utterly alone increased as she went from room to room, and the suffocating silence expanded like a foul mushroom growing in the dark. She called out, but her voice seemed tiny and lost in the emptiness. She searched another room, and another room, until it seemed they would go on into infinity, and all the while she screamed, 'MUM!' but it wasn't a word she could voice or hear. It was trapped in her skull, just as she was trapped in this empty house. Trapped inside her own head and inside this dream . . .

Trapped for ever.

There was a *snick* sound, a shriek, and suddenly she was fully awake and sitting up in bed clutching her blanket in her hands.

For a moment she couldn't get her bearings. She heard a deep panting sound and eventually realized it was her own breathing. She twisted her head round to look at the door. The shrieking was coming from outside, and she thought she could hear someone shouting. She didn't recognize the voice, but then she heard David shouting in response. He sounded shocked and surprised, and his voice was a lot higher than normal.

Penny bolted from her bed, threw open the door and ran out on to the landing.

The first thing she saw was David's white face. He was clutching the handle of a broom so hard that his knuckles were whitening.

'It's not a rat,' he kept saying to her. His jaw was slack, his eyes were wide.

'What?' said Penny. She was completely thrown. She had never seen someone look so frightened.

'It's not a rat,' he said again, and his mouth twitched and he gave a little hysterical yelp.

Penny could hear something to her left, and for some reason she didn't want to turn around and look.

'What's not a rat?' she asked David.

David gave a small queasy smile. He was leaning his head backwards as if trying to escape from some horrid smell. His eyes, which he kept fixed on her, looked glazed as he pointed to the thing to Penny's left, the thing she was still too afraid to look at.

'*That's* not a rat,' he said.

Penny turned. For a moment she couldn't seem to register what she was seeing.

That's OK, she thought to herself. *I'm obviously still dreaming.*

There was a mouse in the rat trap. It was caught by its tail, and it was making 'eek eek' sounds as it struggled to get itself free.

There was also a small brown furry thing which stood on two legs. It was attempting to pull back the trap mechanism in order to free the mouse. The small brown thing couldn't have been much more than two feet tall, and it was most definitely not a rat, because as far as Penny knew, rats didn't go around wearing brown woollen jackets and trousers. Also rats couldn't speak, whereas this small brown thing was clearly using words.

'Still, Mouse, stay still and Pog will set you free,' the brown thing said.

'It's talking,' said David, his voice shaking.

Don't be stupid, David, it's not talking, thought Penny. *This is only a dream.*

Unfortunately, the realization began to dawn on her that she wasn't in fact dreaming. For starters it was too cold on the landing, her legs were starting to tremble, and when she pinched her forearm it genuinely hurt.

'What is it?' David asked.

The small brown thing must have heard David, because it turned around, its eyes flashing with anger. Its lips were pulled back over its needle-sharp teeth, and its furry little jowls wobbled with rage as it snarled: 'You hurt Mouse!'

Penny took a step back, as did David. The creature turned back to the task at hand, and its shoulders shook as it gave one final effort and it pulled the spring back. The mouse darted into the blackness, 'eeking' as it went. The small brown thing let go of the trap and it sprang up in the air. While it was in mid-air the creature batted it out of the way with a paw, and the trap skittered across the landing. The furry creature turned in one fluid movement, pulled a sword from a scabbard strapped to its waist and bent low as if ready to spring.

Despite her shock Penny managed to take in the rest of the creature's attire. It had a waistcoat, a belt, there was a grappling hook strapped to its back, and it held something else in its other hand.

The stick, thought Penny.

The small brown thing growled as it pointed its sword accusingly at them.

Penny could tell from the way the creature's head darted from one side to the other that it was as frightened as it was angry. It trembled all over, and it would have been almost cute if it hadn't been so disconcerting.

The three of them seemed to be at an impasse,

each of them too frightened to do anything.

It was David who finally broke the spell as he suddenly raised the broom over his head, emitted a great 'Raaah!', and rushed the creature.

What happened next made Penny question again whether she was in fact actually awake. David brought the yard brush down, and it hit the ground where the creature had been. David looked confused for a moment. He blinked. There was a hiss to his and Penny's right, and they turned to see the creature now balancing on the banister.

It was as if Penny's eyes had finally caught up with her memory as she remembered a brown blur as the creature had darted out of the way and scaled the banister in less than a second. She had never seen anything move so fast.

David hoisted the brush up again and rushed at the banister.

This time the brush collided with the now-empty banister and rebounded with such force that it bounced back and almost hit him in the head.

The creature was on the wall now. Its paws dug into the plaster and it was snarling at David, its fur standing to attention in rigid spikes as its body trembled.

David rushed it again.

Penny stepped forward and shouted for David to stop. The brush hit the wall, and the bristly head cracked through the old wood and plaster and became wedged there.

The creature leapt on to the floor. It garbled something at them.

David tugged and tugged at the brush, finally wrenching it from the wall. The momentum took him backwards and he fell on to the floor. He was still gripping the handle, and he sat up on his elbows in disbelief.

Both he and Penny watched as the creature took the grappling hook from its back, swung the rope, twirled it until it made a regular swish-swishing sound, and let fly.

The grappling hook flew upwards and caught on the lip of the open attic door. Penny almost admired the flight and form as the rope went from a serpent-like movement to a pleasing tight line as the creature pulled it taut.

They both watched open-mouthed as the creature scaled the rope in less time than it took to blink.

The closing of the attic door almost felt like an insult.

There was nothing they could do. Both Penny

and David could only stand there just gawping upwards.

'What's going on here?'

They both turned to see their father standing on the landing.

Penny stepped forward. 'There was a rat, Dad. We were trying to catch it.'

Her father's eyes went to the hole in the wall, and then to the broom.

'David tried to hit it, but it was too fast. Isn't that right, David?' she said.

She heard David behind her. His response was quiet and still a little stunned. 'What? Yes. What?' he said.

Penny turned to glare at him.

He blinked at her as if waking from a bout of hypnosis and looked at their father. 'Sorry, yes. Sorry, Dad.'

'Don't you think you could have informed me first? Especially before you started vandalizing the house?'

'I don't think it's vandalizing if you actually own the house,' said Penny, immediately regretting her comment when she saw the fury in her father's eyes.

'This is unacceptable!'

Both Penny and David were surprised by the vehemence of their father's reaction.

'It's just . . .' He struggled to find the words, took his glasses off and rubbed the lenses with his dressing gown, then put them back on again. 'Unacceptable.'

For one panicked moment Penny felt the urge to blurt out the truth.

It was a tiny hairy man, Dad. He lives in the attic. He has a fighting stick and a grappling hook. He's like the world's smallest mountain climber.

Her father gestured at the hole in the wall. 'I mean, we've all been through enough without, without . . .' His rage started to fade, and now he seemed at a loss about what to say. He rallied for a moment. 'Just clean this mess up and get back to bed.'

'Right,' said Penny, her lips clamped tightly. Something about what he'd just said had really stung her. *We've all been through enough.* How did a hole in the wall even compare . . . ? She shook herself. 'Yes, Dad. We will.'

He nodded, then turned away and headed back to his bedroom.

Penny nudged David towards her room. They went in, and Penny thought her brother looked pale and drawn. His breathing was ragged after his exertions with the broom.

'Are you all right?'

''Course I'm all right,' said David, sounding offended.

You don't look all right, you look sick and pale, Penny thought, but she kept this to herself.

'What was that thing?' she asked.

'I have no idea,' said David. 'It looked like a gerbil. A walking, talking gerbil. It's not a gerbil though, is it? Unless it's some kind of mutant gerbil. Some kind of mutant gerbil that was created in a lab. A mutant gerbil with climbing tackle, and really bad fashion sense. And it lives in the attic. Our attic. There's a talking mutant gerbil living in our attic!'

'Shut up, David,' Penny snapped. It was the only way to stop his panicked babbling.

David closed his mouth, tight. Then he opened it again as if about to say something. He raised a finger.

'No!' said Penny, glaring at him.

David seemed to reconsider, and eventually he lowered his hand. 'What are we going to do?' he asked plaintively.

'Well, we know it can talk,' said Penny.

David shook his head slowly. 'We're not going to—'

'We are,' said Penny.

David shook his head more vigorously.

Penny grinned. She felt cold, but tingly, as if she'd just been shocked into life.

Pog was enraged. He paced back and forth across the attic, casting occasional glances at the door, while keeping his right paw on the hilt of his sword.

He wasn't really sure he was going to use his sword. In fact, he'd felt his resolve melt as soon as he'd touched it.

Pog sighed and let his hand fall by his side.

Then the rage came again, and he growled and kicked a stray piece of wood across the floor.

'Stupid Pog. Stupid. Stupidest of all. Pog is supposed to stay hidden,' he ranted to himself. He could feel a sour thickness in his throat, and even in his rage he knew tears weren't far away. 'Stupid,' he said again huskily, and wiped a paw across his eyes.

He finally dropped to the ground and sat with his back to his den. He lowered his head, and looked at the floorboards. Once again, he'd revealed himself to the tall folk despite the fact that he was supposed to stay hidden.

'Sorry, Grandfa,' he sniffled.

The dark closed in around him.

CHAPTER
16

Penny and David waited until they were sure their father would be fully asleep again. Then they crept out the back door and to the shed with two torches. The night sky was cloudless, and it was surprisingly chilly. Penny clutched her dressing gown to herself, while David simply walked out in his pyjamas and shoes. The cold didn't seem to bother him and Penny decided that there was no point in reprimanding him for not wearing a jacket, and risking another 'You're not Mum' comment.

They managed to wrestle the ladder from the shed after much twisting and turning and arguing with each other over who had which end, and who wasn't turning it in the right direction. Eventually they manoeuvred it out the door. Then came the difficulties involved in trying to get it into the house and up the stairs without thumping it on every step, like they had done the last time. They spent the time hissing at each other in the dark, until finally they got it up on to the landing and had it pointed at the attic door.

'Ready?' asked Penny.

'Ready,' said David, looking upwards and licking his lips.

They pushed. Penny winced at the dull clump as the ladder hit the attic door. The scraping noise that followed as they used the ladder to shove the door upwards only made her wince all the more. She wasn't sure whether it was the combination of the excruciating sound, the fact that it might wake her father, or the fact that she half expected something to dive at them from the dark above, which made her feel this way.

She let out a great whoosh of relief when they got the ladder in place.

'Right then,' she said.

David looked at her. She looked at him. David raised his arm pathetically towards the ladder.

Penny sighed: 'Fine, I'll go first.'

She put her foot on the first rung, and was about to move on up when she heard David whisper behind her.

'We should bring a stick,' he said.

Penny turned back to look at him. 'Why? Because trying to hit it with something worked so well the first time?'

'No need to be sarcastic,' he said.

Penny turned back to the ladder. She steeled herself for a moment and, fixing her eyes on a point in the middle distance, she started her ascent. She reckoned it was best not to think about what she was doing. There was no sense in thinking about how insane this all seemed, or how at any moment she might be accosted by a very angry furry ball. She paused for a moment and closed her eyes. She remembered an evening from a few years back when they'd all gone to her school's art exhibition. Penny had stood waiting as the winners were announced, her heart pounding, terrified that she would be called, terrified that she might trip and fall on the way up to the podium, the panic rising in her.

Then she'd felt the pressure on her shoulders. Her mother's hands, strong and reassuring. 'It'll be fine, Pen. It'll all be fine,' she'd whispered. The calm that had settled over her was so soothing she'd felt like she could do anything.

When they'd called her name she'd strode up to collect her prize. Knowing her mother was smiling and applauding her had given her a strength she'd never dreamt she had.

She opened her eyes and climbed up quickly. She reached the top and started to move the door aside with the splayed fingers of her hand. There was that scraping sound, not as bad as nails on a blackboard, but not so low that it wasn't irritating. She peered into the darkness.

'Careful,' said David.

'I am being careful,' she hissed back at him.

She pushed the panel aside enough to make room for herself to enter. She tried to switch her torch on, surprised by the fact that she had suddenly lost complete control of her fingers. She flicked it on, almost dropping it in the process.

'You're shaking the ladder,' said David.

Penny rolled her eyes. Then she shone the torch up into the dark maw of the attic, pulling her head back in expectation of an attack.

'Anything?' asked David.

'No,' she said curtly.

There was only one thing for it. She grabbed the lip of the attic entrance and hoisted herself in. She sat on the edge with her legs dangling downward and scanned the attic quickly with her torch. Nothing moved. She looked down at David.

'Come on,' she said.

Without waiting for his reply she pulled her legs in and bounced into a standing position. David raced up the ladder and grunted as he pulled himself into the attic and on to his knees. He dropped his torch and it went rolling across the floor, sending light spinning across the floor and walls and causing a rumbling sound. Penny stepped forward and stood on it to stop it moving any further. She gave David an accusing look.

David just shrugged in response. He grabbed his torch, mumbled a very half-hearted thank you, and dusted himself off as he stood up.

They both shone their torches around the room. There wasn't any pattern to their probing, and both knew that it was more out of fear and a need to banish the dark than a quest to find something.

'See anything?' asked Penny, knowing it was a pointless question, but feeling the need to say something.

'Nope,' said David.

By 'nope', Penny could tell what he really meant was, 'Can we go back down now?'

But Penny wasn't going to be deterred. She walked further into the attic and headed for the far wall. David followed, looking behind him as he went. They checked the walls and ceiling. They checked the floor. They found nothing.

'He could have gone out through the roof,' David whispered.

Penny nodded, then she marched purposefully towards the rocking horse. She circled it and bent under it. There was nothing but mildew and cobwebs, but Penny was beginning to find her courage, and a new sense of purpose. She pointed at the makeshift den in the corner. 'Let's have a look at that.'

They both headed towards it. David seemed to be drawing courage from Penny, and they almost stomped across the floor, as if their belligerence might frighten their intruder and let him know they meant business.

David bent down and started to reach towards the den. 'Look at all this. It's like—'

A shrieking shadow dropped from the rafter above their heads.

David was hit full force in the chest, and reeled backwards as if he'd been hit by a bullet. His torch flew out of his hand. The creature hit the ground, tumbled over and came to a stop, crouching defensively with its stick held aloft in its paw and a sword in the other.

'Pog's!' it shouted.

Penny stepped forward with one hand raised to placate the creature.

It took a step back, then took a step forward, snarling, its panicked eyes darting from one to the other.

Penny knew how the creature felt. She too was terrified, but a strange calm was also descending upon her. She looked to where a wheezing David was picking himself up off the floor. He was rubbing his chest. Penny nodded at him, her hand still held palm up in creature's direction. David winced, but he nodded back in understanding to let her know he was OK. Penny turned back to the furry thing.

'What's Pog's?' she said.

'This! This!' said the creature, turning its staff in a circle to mark its territory.

'Who's Pog?' asked Penny, surprised by the calm in her own voice.

'I is Pog!' it said, jutting its jaw out defiantly.

'You're Pog?' said Penny. The creature – *he* – had a name?

The creature's eyes lit up with rage. 'That's what Pog said. Pog is Pog! Is girl-one deaf?'

David came and stood beside Penny and kept

rubbing his chest. 'That hurt.'

Pog glared at him. 'Well then, boy-one shouldn't have been poking around in what doesn't belong to him.'

'*Boy-one* has a name too,' said David, taking a step towards Pog.

Pog took a step towards David. 'Boy-one doesn't deserve a name. Names is for honourable ones.'

David started forward again, but Penny put a restraining hand on his forearm.

'We're sorry, Pog,' she said.

David looked at her as if she'd lost her mind.

Pog suddenly looked crestfallen. He started to pace back and forth and slap the palms of his hands against his temples. 'No, no, is all wrong. Pog is revealed, and his promise will be revealed, and all is wrong.'

Penny and David shared a bemused look. A very agitated Pog was now going round and round in circles.

Penny shook her head. 'We don't know of any promise.'

Pog kept frowning at her, then slowly his face slackened as if something was dawning on him. He looked sideways over his left shoulder, as if listening to someone standing behind him.

'What's that?' he said. There was a long pause, and he started to nod. 'That's right, Grandfa. Pog will do his best, even though he is revealed.'

A worried-looking Pog started to tap his right foot on the floor.

Her fear was gone, and now Penny was beginning to feel sorry for the creature. She had no idea what this *promise* was, but she could see how upset Pog was about it.

'Whatever this promise is, we won't tell anyone about it. In fact, you don't even have to tell us what it is. We won't tell anyone anything about you,' she said.

Pog looked up at her and tilted his head. 'What's that she says?'

'We won't tell a soul about you,' smiled Penny. She hoped her smile was encouraging.

Pog seemed to consider this.

David sighed. 'That's right. We won't tell anyone, little hairy man gerbil.' He started to bend over and speak very slowly. 'We won't tell. Cross our hearts.'

Pog curled his lip in disdain. 'Why you talking slow, like Pog is stupid? Pog isn't stupid. Pog is brightest of the bright. Grandfa even says. And Pog is Pog. Pog is named, and Pog knows the Lore, like all Lumpkins.' Pog thumped his chest. 'Pog is Pog, big hairless boy-thing.' He looked David up and down with contempt.

David wasn't having any of it. 'Well, David is David. Do you hear that? David is David.'

'Pog is Pog.'

'David is David.'

'Pog is Pog.'

'David is—'

'Shut up, both of you!' Penny shouted.

They both looked taken aback by her outburst.

Penny sighed. 'We need to talk.'

'Quietly,' said David. 'Because in fairness, Pen, that was a little loud, and we don't want to wake Dad again.'

Pog tilted his head as if listening, then he shook it. 'Pog's hearing is good. No movement from the tall one. The tall one sleeps too deep and won't be woken. The tall one is dreaming and speaks of . . .' Pog frowned, one ear twitched . . . 'Ellen.'

It was like being suddenly slapped in the face. Penny didn't have to look at David to know that he'd experienced the same shock. She could see the look of puzzlement on Pog's face. One of his eyes narrowed.

'What did Pog say to give youse pause?' he asked.

Penny gave a fragile smile. 'Nothing,' she said. 'It's

just like you said, you must have really good hearing.' *Yes*, she thought. *Your hearing must be really good to be able to tell that our dad is dreaming, and that even in his sleep he's calling our mum's name.*

Pog puffed his chest out. 'Pog has the best hearing of all. Grandfa is always saying.'

'Who's Grandfa?' asked Penny.

Now it was Pog's turn to look deflated. His shoulders sank, and he looked at the floor. There was silence.

'I need to sit down,' said David. He lowered himself on to the floor and sat cross-legged, looking at the empty space between his knees. He rubbed his chest again.

'Pog is sorry about David-is-David's chest.'

'It's just David,' said David.

'Pog is sorry about Just-David's chest.'

'No, not Just-David.'

Pog frowned. 'Not-Just-David? Pog is getting confused now. How many names—'

Penny interjected before things got too out of hand. 'His name is *David*. And tell me, what are you, Pog?'

Penny was surprised by the way things had changed. Here they were conversing with this strange little creature when moments before they'd both been terrified. Yet when you started talking to him, despite the fact that she couldn't believe he existed, he actually seemed quite reasonable. She was beginning to marvel at her own ability to accept things.

'Pog is of the First Folk,' said Pog, with an air of incredulity which suggested he couldn't even fathom why Penny had asked such a question.

'First Folk? Who are they?' asked David.

'First Folk. We was here first before the tall folk. First Folk lived in the Burrows in the forest, lived all over.'

'We've never seen any First Folk,' said Penny.

Pog grinned and tapped the side of his head. 'That's 'cause First Folk takes care to be hexed invisible. Never to be seen. Hidden deep and aways, and sideways. Scattered now, somewhat.' He mumbled the last few words and looked troubled.

'I didn't think creatures like you even existed,' said David.

Pog was bemused. 'First Folk not exist?' He started to spread his arms wide, as if presenting himself on stage just before launching into singing some great operatic aria. 'Pog is here, isn't he?'

Penny smiled. 'Yes, Pog is most definitely here.'

Pog smiled at her, and Penny was surprised but

delighted when she felt her heart leap at the sight.

'Where are the other First Folk?' asked Penny, both she and Pog now smiling at each other like old friends.

Pog's face crumpled. Penny felt a sudden jolt of guilt when she saw his look of utter devastation. Pog rubbed a paw along the shaft of the stick, and his eyes searched the floor. His voice was quiet and husky.

'Scattered, like Pog already said. Scattered since the Burrows fell.'

'The Burrows?' said Penny.

Pog ran a hand agitatedly over his head. 'Pog's home.'

Penny frowned. 'But if it's your home, why are you—'

'Pog must hold to his promise now. Pog must stay here and not go forth and return to his people until his task is done,' he snapped.

He kept looking at the floor, and Penny exchanged a glance with David. He'd noticed the change in Pog's demeanour too, but he was just as lost as Penny was.

Penny bent down towards him. Her voice was low and gentle. 'What was the promise, Pog?'

Pog turned his head and looked at her. Penny

marvelled at his liquid–brown eyes. Even in the gloom of the attic they were full of light, and despite his bouts of fierceness, Penny could feel herself warming to him. He seemed terribly vulnerable and alone.

'The promise is old,' said Pog. 'The promise means that Pog must hold the Necessary, for to look after and protect like those who came before him.'

On the word 'protect', Pog stood more erect and grasped his staff with both hands and slammed it twice against his chest.

'The Necessary?' said Penny.

Pog nodded. Penny was about to follow up with another question, but David interrupted: 'Was it you who stacked all those books in the study?'

Pog nodded again. He looked pleased with himself, and he gave a broad smile, catching himself unawares. He seemed to think he'd let his guard down because he suddenly became embarrassed. His smile vanished and he lowered his head and toed a knot in the wooden floor.

'How long have you been here, Pog?' asked Penny.

'Long enough,' Pog said in a low voice without raising his head. 'Since' — he cleared his throat — 'since it was Grandfa's duty to guard the Necessary. It passed to Pog when Grandfa ... since Grandfa ...'

Pog seemed to be struggling now. Penny thought he looked on the verge of tears.

'Your grandfather, you mean?' she asked.

Pog nodded briskly, avoiding her eyes.

'Is your grandfa gone?' said Penny quietly.

'He died,' said David, a strange blank tone to his voice.

'Gave his life for First Folk and tall folk alike, did Grandfa,' said Pog. He looked fiercely and proudly at both of them, but his chin was trembling.

Penny bent down on one knee before him. 'Then you should do what he did and keep the promise, Pog. You should look after and protect, just as he did. Maybe we could help you.'

Pog straightened himself up. 'This Pog will do then.' He frowned for a moment, then he shuffled forward and leant in sideways to Penny. 'The tall one? Him that dreams? What of him?'

Penny smiled. 'We won't say anything to him.'

Pog looked sceptical.

'Ever,' said Penny.

Pog seemed to consider what she was saying. Penny reached out her hand. Pog looked at it, then shook it. He grinned.

Penny smiled. 'I'm Penny, and this is my brother David.'

Pog nodded at David. David raised his hand slightly, looking a little awkward about the whole exchange.

'David,' said Pog. 'Not Not–Just–David.'

'No, not Not–Just–David,' Penny laughed.

David shook his head and gave a wry grin.

Pog patted his stick against his chest. 'Pog Lumpkin of the Burrows to the North, before the Far Reaches.'

'Right,' said Penny. She was completely befuddled by Pog's strange talk, but she was still smiling. All previous fear and trepidation was gone now. She decided that she liked Pog, and for the first time in months she felt something like happiness.

They left a much happier Pog in the attic and headed for the shed. David didn't say a word to his sister as they returned the ladder. He was scratching the palm of his hand as they exited the shed.

'If you scratch it, it won't heal,' she said.

David snorted.

Penny ignored him as she locked the padlock on the shed door.

'Don't you think he's a bit odd?' David said. He was looking at her furtively, as if he was afraid Pog might hear him. He had the tips of his fingers on his left hand grazing the palm of his right. Penny gave him a pointed look, and he sighed and took his hand away.

'He seems fine to me,' she said.

'He was talking to thin air at one point, Pen.'

'He was talking to his grandfa,' said Penny. 'Haven't you ever . . . ?'

David looked at her warily. 'What? Haven't I ever what?'

Penny shrugged it off. 'Nothing.'

'There's a talking rat in our attic who has conversations with himself. You don't think that's a bit strange?'

'He's First Folk,' said Penny.

'Oh, right, like that's a proper—'

Penny raised an eyebrow, and waited for him to finish his sentence.

'You know what I mean,' said a flustered David.

Penny shook her head. 'No, I don't.' She sighed. 'He's fine, David. He's a friend, I can tell. Besides, he said he was here to protect.'

David looked at her. He didn't say anything. He didn't need to. Penny had already thought the same thing.

Protect from what?

Penny pulled her dressing gown around her.

'Come on, let's go inside. It's cold out here.'

They trudged back to the house. Penny was tired despite the strangeness and excitement of the night. She said goodnight to a bleary-eyed David as he went into his room. He half-heartedly raised a hand in response and didn't look round.

Penny was alone on the landing now. She looked up at the attic door. 'You can probably hear me, Pog, can't you?' she whispered. 'I know. You said your hearing was good. I just wanted to say again that I promise we won't tell anyone about you, especially Dad.'

Penny waited for a moment, but she didn't hear anything. She went into her room and closed the door behind her.

Up in the attic, a sleeping Pog nestled in his den. His ears and mouth twitched as he gave a contented smile.

'Well, who wants to come with me?'

Dad was standing by the door, twisting his car keys around the fingers of one hand, his eyebrows raised as he looked at Penny and David. Penny felt the familiar flicker of panic when she saw his car keys. She had to bite her lip in an effort to stop herself asking him to be careful.

David looked at him with suspicion. 'You're going to an antiques shop?'

Dad nodded eagerly, and tried to smile. Penny scanned his eyes; they looked grey and weary, and his beard was going to silver. His T-shirt seemed too big for him, and he was stooping slightly. He seemed as brittle as bird bones. Penny wanted to ask him if he was OK. She wanted to tell him about

Pog. She wanted to ask him what did he dream about.

In the end she just shook her head and gave a weak smile. 'No thanks, Dad.'

'It's just to get a couple of things to brighten the house up,' he said.

Penny shifted from one foot to the other. David cleared his throat and looked anywhere else but in the direction of his father.

'Right,' their dad said. He took in a deep breath and let it out. 'I won't be long.'

Penny's heart almost skipped a beat when she heard those words. Both she and David knew that when their father said 'I won't be long', it usually meant at least an hour. He had a terrible habit of getting distracted and popping into different shops on his way to his main destination, particularly antiques shops. Penny had seen at least two antiques shops in the village on their way here, and she knew that her dad would be driven by the urge to visit both of them.

It was armed with this knowledge that Penny and David found themselves moments later on the landing, looking up at the attic door. They stood there for a few seconds as if afraid to do or say anything. It was almost as if they feared breaking some sort of spell. The previous night had seemed like a dream, and Penny wondered if they were both afraid to prove to themselves that it had been an actual dream. She could feel herself holding her breath. Her chest and shoulders were tight with tension. Eventually David just sighed and nodded at her and said, 'Go on then.'

Penny cleared her throat. 'Pog,' she whispered.

It seemed the word was too light and Penny could feel a strange sensation, as if she'd thrown feathers up in the air, only for her heart to sink as she watched them float downwards to the ground. She tried again, this time a little louder.

'Pog,' she said.

There was nothing for a moment.

Then Penny's heart fluttered in her chest as she saw the attic door lift a crack, and two small glittering eyes peeked down at them.

'What's to do now?' asked Pog.

'Pog!' said Penny, with such delight that David looked embarrassed to be near her.

Pog poked his head out further from the gloom, and wrinkled his nose. 'Yes, Pog is here.'

'Come down, Pog,' said Penny.

Pog frowned, and his eyes met Penny's. Penny smiled.

That seemed to sway Pog, because in the next moment he had dropped down a coil of rope and had descended in the amount of time it took to draw breath.

Pog looked up at Penny and David, blinking at them in the light.

Penny bent over him with her palms on her thighs. The sense of airy delight she felt on seeing Pog again almost made her giddy. In daylight, Pog's face seemed even more animated. His furry features twitched and rippled as he went through a whole series of emotions in a few seconds flat. He seemed apprehensive, nervous, wary. The wariness gave way to curiosity, and the curiosity became something else as he took a step towards Penny. Then the best thing of all happened, and Penny thought her heart would burst.

Pog smiled.

'Penny,' he said.

'Pog,' said Penny.

David rolled his eyes.

Penny leant over Pog again. 'Would you like to come downst—'

Like a whip being cracked, Pog was off. He was a blur of speed as he leapt up and slid down the banister, landing on the floor of the hallway below with a satisfying thump. He looked up at David and Penny:

'Who woulds like to follow Pog?'

They followed Pog downstairs, and when they reached the bottom, Pog looked at David and tapped the side of his head. 'Pog hasn't forgotten that you hurt Mouse.' David looked slightly uncomfortable on being reminded of this fact, and Pog looked thoughtful. 'But David was protecting. Pog understands. So David can be forgiven.'

Pog smiled at David, and a relieved-looking David returned his smile. Penny could feel herself warming to Pog more and more.

'What's to do now, Pog?' she asked.

'Pog will do what Pog does and guard the Necessary.'

'The Necessary. You keep mentioning that. What is it?'

Pog seemed to consider things for a moment. Then, clasping his paws together, he seemed to come to a decision.

'Best not to say. Best to show,' said Pog. He beckoned them down the hallway.

Part of Penny wasn't surprised when she realized he was leading them towards the cellar door. She felt that odd feeling again, as if shifting from one world where all was clear and defined to one where things were slightly muffled, as if everything – sound, sensation and light – was wrapped in cotton wool.

They reached the door. Pog gestured towards the symbol at its base. He turned to them and smiled. 'This meaning is clear. The Necessary is locked and scissioned.'

Penny looked at David. He frowned at her and shook his head.

'That symbol,' said Penny, pointing at the base of the door, 'gives me a headache.'

''Course,' said Pog. ''Tis a warding glyph. It pushes. Sends nosy ones away.'

'It's not completely successful though, is it? I mean, we're standing here looking at it,' said Penny.

Pog stroked his chin. 'True enough. Penny and David have come closest. Most others avoid the Necessary. Most never make it down the hallway.'

'How do you open it?' asked David.

Pog's eyes widened. 'Pog almost mostly never opens it. The Necessary must remain locked.'

'Why?' asked David.

'Things come through,' said Pog.

'What things?' said David.

Pog just patted the door.

'Almost mostly never?' said Penny, with a raised eyebrow.

Pog looked at her.

'That means you do open it sometimes.' Penny smiled.

'Could you open it now?' asked David.

Pog blinked rapidly. 'What's that?'

'Could you open it?' Penny asked.

Pog started to shuffle slightly, and his fingers worked together fretfully. 'Now then, 'tisn't safe.'

'Are you sure? We only want a quick look,' said Penny.

Pog looked wary, but Penny noticed the doubt in his eyes.

'If you open it sometimes, then that must mean it is safe sometimes,' she said.

Pog seemed to reconsider. He muttered to himself. 'Quietest during the day. 'Tis only at night that things come and try to pass through.' Pog finally nodded to himself, then looked at Penny and David. 'A moment so, but only a moment.'

Penny felt a little ripple of excitement.

'Do you have a key?' asked David.

'A key? A key, David says?' said Pog, looking highly amused. He unstrapped his staff from his back and held it two-handed, parallel with the floor, and pressed it against the door.

David and Penny exchanged a look, and Penny was about to say something when the runes on Pog's staff started to glow a brilliant white, and the whole hallway started to hum.

'What's that?' David gasped.

''Tis the Necessary opening,' said Pog, concentrating on the door.

The door itself now started to shimmer with a white luminescence, until very soon Penny and David had to shield their eyes.

Just as they thought the brightness was becoming too much, it suddenly winked out of existence.

The door was gone.

There was an opening where it had been. It led out on to a marshy plain fringed by bare trees. Sickly-looking clouds slid across the sky, turning it a dirty smoky grey. As a breeze blew in through the opening, they smelt a sour stench. Both of them covered their noses.

A dizzy Penny started to look around her in an attempt to orient herself, but try as she might, she couldn't grasp the fact that the cellar door was looking out on to somewhere that shouldn't exist.

'Where is that?' she asked.

'Someplace else,' said Pog.

'A good place?' asked David, and it was clear from the slight tremble in his voice that he already knew the answer.

Pog's eyes narrowed, and he looked grimly out on to the dead landscape. He shook his head, leant on his staff with both hands and shifted his weight. 'Once, long ago, even before tall folk came here, the first of the First Folk sensed an opening from another world. A crack 'tween this place and some-place else. Things came through. Bad things. Horrid things. The first of the First Folk fought the monsters what passed through, and using the Lore the crack was sealed.'

Pog raised himself up proudly.

'From thence, a Lumpkin was always assigned as Keeper of the Necessary, to guard against ingress, to stop the monsters from gaining a hold in this world.'

Penny looked out into the wasteland. A feeling of dread descended on her so powerfully that she felt the irrational urge to run.

'But if your people sealed it, why do things keep getting through?' she asked.

Pog sighed. 'Magicks were worked, but they's weakening as time passes. Now things squeeze through.' He looked at them both and saw their nervousness. 'On occasion,' he added hurriedly.

'It's like an old plaster,' said Penny.

'A what now?' asked Pog.

'A sticking plaster,' said Penny. 'It's getting weaker with age.'

'How weak will it eventually get?' asked David.

Pog patted the frame where the door had been. 'Strong the Necessary is, always.' He shuffled nervously. 'Always.'

'Pog?' said Penny.

Pog tried to look her in the eyes and failed.

'Always?' said Penny.

Pog bit his lower lip. 'Once ago, long after the first ingress, something else came through. A great evil. Powerful. It led creatures here, and the First Folk fought a second terrible battle. The Necessary was damaged, but there were those who healed it, and the evil was banished.' Pog swallowed hard, and his voice was husky. He lowered his eyes. 'Many were lost.'

'Including Grandfa?' asked Penny.

Pog nodded, but he wouldn't look up. Penny bowed down in front of him and tilted his face up. There were tears in his eyes.

'I'm so sorry, Pog,' she said.

Pog nodded in gratitude and wiped a hand across

his eyes. He took in a deep breath. 'Best to close it now.'

He stood before the opening and jabbed the staff towards the entrance. The shimmering began again. Penny was shocked when David suddenly grabbed her forearm.

'Pen! Look!'

It was hard to see through the ever-increasing brightness, but by the trees on the horizon Penny could make out dark shapes. Long, slow undulating shapes that seemed to be rolling towards them. The back of her neck prickled with heat, and David's hand squeezed harder.

Hurry, Pog. Hurry, was all she could think.

The door reappeared, and Pog stood back and gave an 'Ah' of satisfaction. Penny ballooned her cheeks and pushed out a relieved breath. David let go of her arm.

'Sealed and safe now. No ingress here,' smiled Pog.

Penny looked at the edges of the door. She was convinced there were more cracks now. Pog noticed her look of concern, and he gave the door a hearty slap.

'No ingress,' he repeated.

He was smiling, but Penny saw the flicker of doubt in his eyes.

A sticking plaster, she thought. *It's just a sticking plaster.*

They walked back down the hallway. Pog seemed to have grown in stature a little since revealing his secret.

'How does that stick work?' asked David.

''Tis a staff,' said Pog, looking slightly offended. 'A staff handed down from Lumpkin to Lumpkin. It remembers.'

'It what?' said David, stopping in surprise.

'Remembers, holds memories from those who did wield it. 'Tis what gives it its power.' Pog spun the staff around like a marching baton. ''Tis a key, a weapon – it glows with memories of those who came before. Within the wood and runes are those—'

Pog stopped himself for a moment and his eyes seemed to be elsewhere.

'Those who came before or some small part of 'em,' he said quietly. He suddenly straightened up and beckoned them on. 'Pog will explain.'

They followed him as he scampered towards the sitting room.

As they entered the room, Pog stood before the fireplace, looking up at the urn.

'What's that now?' asked Pog, pointing up to the urn.

'That's M–Mum,' said Penny, stumbling over the first 'M', hating herself for the way the word came out like a muffled yelp.

Pog's eyes narrowed. 'Mum? Like Ma?'

'Yes,' said Penny. 'It's another way of saying *mother*.'

Pog frowned. 'Penny and David's ma?'

They both nodded.

'In there?' said Pog, pointing upwards.

'Well, yes, sort of . . . it's hard to . . .' Penny didn't know how to answer. Her mouth was dry. She licked her lips.

Pog nodded for a moment, then said brightly: 'It remembers!'

'What?' said Penny.

'It remembers,' said Pog, 'the way what Grandfa's staff does.' Pog rubbed his chin as he looked up at the urn. 'Take Mum down from there.'

'Why?' Penny asked.

'Take Mum down,' said Pog gently, fixing her with a look that was kind but firm.

Penny nodded and stepped towards the mantel-piece. She gently took the urn in her hands, terrified that it might slip because her palms were sweating so much. She placed it on a table by a bookcase, and when Pog saw this was accomplished, he closed his eyes and smiled and nodded to himself.

'What's going on?' David asked.

Pog tilted his head as he studied the urn in its new location. 'Best to have Mum closer. That which remembers must always be held close.' Pog stepped towards the urn and he swept his hands over it gently, as if feeling for the faintest trace of cobwebs. 'We looks at things and holds them close. Things what remind us of family. Powerful they become. Memories of those who have gone before, laid down they are, like layers of silt on riverbeds – and they sway, this way and that with the current, and we hold, and we remember. 'Tis our duty to remember.'

Penny was holding her breath. She looked at David. He was barely moving; his eyes were transfixed on what Pog was doing.

Pog turned to them both. His eyes were glittering with tears, but he smiled:

'Them that's dead is never gone.'

PART
3

Boggarts, Belches
and Bane

CHAPTER 18

Penny and David and their father had gone to something called 'the super market'. It had been a couple of days since his confession, and the guilt Pog felt about revealing the Necessary was gnawing away at him. It was his choice as Keeper, but he still wondered if it had been the right thing to do. He was a bit ashamed when he realized he might have just been showing off. He hadn't heard Grandfa's voice since that day, and he wondered if that was Grandfa's way of showing his disapproval.

Grandfa is gone, said another voice.

Pog rubbed his nose agitatedly and gave a long hard sniff. 'Quiet now. Pog is thinking,' he said to the darkness in the attic.

He tried to ignore the words, but there was

no denying the sudden ache in his chest. He blinked his eyes; they were stinging, as if irritated by smoke.

Smoke and fire, Pog, said the insidious voice. *Smoke and fire and screams. Remember?*

'Hush now,' Pog shouted.

His voice echoed in the dark. Pog felt suddenly alone. He tried to think of something else.

Penny.

Penny was nice.

Penny was always smiling and friendly, but Pog noticed that there was also suspicion clouding her eyes when she asked him questions. It hadn't helped that whenever they spoke these days, Pog couldn't seem to keep still. He moved from one foot to the other, and always found himself looking towards the nearest window. One day he'd scampered up to the kitchen sink, his hackles raised, while Penny was mid-sentence. He'd wrinkled his snout and sniffed the air. 'Something's up!' he'd shouted all of a sudden, surprising even himself. He supposed it was instinct, and that he just couldn't help himself. He'd turned around slowly to find both Penny and David gawping at him.

'What's up, Pog?' Penny had asked.

Pog panicked. 'Rain,' he'd said brightly.

The sun was blazing outside. Penny and David looked bemused.

Pog gestured back towards the window. 'Soon. Quite soon ... maybe ... rain. Pog knows ...' he said weakly, and he turned his face away and tried to think of something else to say.

The truth was, there was indeed something on the air. He couldn't place it, but it was a raw, sour scent. It came from the forest, particularly at night, moving from one spot to the next as if something was probing for an opening. But nothing had passed through the Necessary recently. Pog would have known. Some nights Pog found himself in the kitchen, his right hand gripping Grandfa's staff fiercely, snarling to himself, his snout quivering, and him muttering, 'Pog is here. Pog is waiting. Come to Pog if you dares.'

But nothing came, and the smell shifted and changed, and sometimes disappeared altogether.

'Something's up, Mouse,' he said, shaking his index finger. 'And Pog will found out what it is.'

Pog climbed up the attic wall and crawled up on to the ceiling. He squeezed between a gap in the tiles and wriggled out on to the roof.

He sniffed the air. There was a scent on it, one that shouldn't be there, and he thought he heard something faint on the breeze.

'What's this now?'

This was different to the strange scent he couldn't place. This was something familiar.

Pog climbed down from the roof and headed across the road and into the forest. The smell was stronger here, and the sound he heard was getting louder. Pog's heart started to quicken – and the sight of something moving by a tree made it pound.

Pog pulled up just before the tree. There was a badger nuzzling something at the base of the tree. She was chittering agitatedly, and as Pog slowly stepped forward he saw she was nudging the corpse of another badger. The badger nuzzling her fallen mate turned and hissed at Pog, her eyes red-rimmed with grief and rage. Pog held a hand up.

'Easy now. Pog is here to help.'

Slowly the badger moved aside. Pog knelt before her mate. The badger was cold and lifeless; blood matted his grey fur and his eyes were glassy. The badger had clearly been ripped apart by teeth and claws. Pog patted his fur, and said, 'There there, now,' all the while feeling utterly useless.

He helped the badger bury her fallen mate. A squirrel slipped along the branch of a tree and watched them, followed quickly by another. Pog looked up at them, hardly seeing them through his tears of rage. 'Pog will find who did this, and Pog will make them pay,' he said hoarsely.

When his task was completed the badger nuzzled and licked the palm of Pog's hand, then she turned and waddled off into the forest. Pog watched her go, clenching his fists and wiping his eyes.

'Pog will find who did this,' he said again.

He made his way back to the house, fury tightening every muscle of his body.

Smoke and fire and screams.

Pog shook his head. *Enough*, he thought to himself. He climbed back up into the attic.

Mouse was scuttling around in a corner. Pog sat cross-legged with his staff in his lap and looked at him. He tried to say something about what he'd seen in the forest, but he suddenly felt terribly weary.

The car was loaded up with shopping. It was when they were about a mile from the house that Penny decided to ask her dad the question. She'd been trying to ask it for ages, and now she was fit to bursting. It was passing through the village that had finally decided it for her. In particular it was the last building they'd passed on the way out that had brought it to mind.

'Have you decided on a new school for us, Dad?'

David's head whipped around and he gave her an incredulous look. Penny ignored him.

'School? It's the summer holidays, and you're asking about school?' Dad said, giving a half-hearted chuckle.

'It's just . . . we should probably start looking soon, and besides, we missed a couple of months. We haven't been back since . . .'

This time David looked at Penny with real fury. She saw her dad's shoulders stiffen and he just ever so slightly pushed his back into the seat.

Since Mum died since Mum died since Mum died. The phrase kept going around and around in Penny's head.

The atmosphere in the car had changed. There was a hot silence that just seemed to stretch on and on.

'Look, Penny—'

Penny couldn't help herself. She felt a quick sting of anger. 'Dad, listen, I just want to know—'

'When you're ready I'll start asking arou—'

'We are ready. Once summer is over . . .'

His hands tightened on the steering wheel. She could see the white points of his knuckles.

'I'll decide when—'

'It's just that you need to start looking. It's really not fair—'

Her dad exploded. He never shouted at them, but he shouted now, and the sound of it inside the confined space of the car made their ears ring.

'Not fair? *Not fair?* Well, I think if life has taught us anything in the last few months it's that life is *not fair.*'

Penny was stunned into silence. She had no idea what to say. She tried to look at David, but he was twisted away from her in his seat, looking out the window.

'Nice one,' he whispered.

No one said another word for the rest of the journey.

Pog was downstairs. In the attic, he was only brooding about the incident in the forest, so he thought patrolling downstairs might take his mind off it.

The house was quiet now, but different. Not the quiet that he was used to when he was alone in the dark. That was a warm, mothy quiet that wrapped itself around him and felt part of him. This was a quiet that made him realize now that he was somehow separate from the house, that he was different, that his world was now different.

And it was all because the children weren't here. He suddenly felt exposed in the vastness of the house in a way he never had before.

Pog scratched his head. Thinking about it made him feel strange. He hadn't felt like this before they came. He'd been happy in his way, although he had been alone. Feeling alone only became more intense after the little girl had gone. Now the Cresswells were here and he didn't feel alone any more, and when they weren't here there was an edge to things, as if the world had become sharp and unfriendly. He realized he liked it more now when they were here. He mused on all of this as he headed to the Necessary.

Pog's eyes were drawn to the cracks that surrounded the border of the door. He couldn't swear to it, but he thought they seemed to be getting bigger. There seemed to be more every day, popping up all over the house. Pog had heard Penny and David's father say something about a thing called 'subsidence'. Pog had shaken his head and pursed his lips when he heard this. This was something else, and again it seemed to have got worse since the Cresswells had moved in.

Cracks were not good. Cracks meant things were crumbling.

'Sticking plaster,' said Pog, as he trailed a finger along one of the cracks nearest the floor. For a moment he thought he smelt something mucky and wet, but the smell was gone in seconds.

'It holds,' he said to reassure himself.

Pog made his way to the sitting room. The urn was still standing on the table. Pog ambled towards it. The surface was dull and scratched. Pog sniffed the urn, and once again wondered how 'Mum' could be in there. The children didn't say it in so many words, but Pog knew for a fact now that Mum was gone from this world.

'Gone to a good place most likely,' Pog said to himself, and he smiled. Pog thought that those who were of Mum and with Mum were good and decent, so she must have been good and decent too.

Pog pursed his lips and narrowed his eyes. He was still for a moment, then he suddenly dashed towards the kitchen. He rummaged under the kitchen sink and came out with a cloth. He dashed back to the sitting room and set to work polishing the urn. He polished with speed and care, fogging the surface with his breath, polishing greasy spots until they shone a bright brassy glow. When he was finished, Pog stood back and admired his handiwork.

The sun shone in through the sitting-room window and the urn gleamed. Pog smiled even more. His smile started to fade when he smelt the smell again. Something wet and sour. His fur stood on end, and Pog felt a presence behind him. He slowly reached for his staff and turned around.

Something black, shining wetly, was slithering into the sitting room.

'Bloodworm,' Pog hissed.

The long eel-like creature had no head, but it had a mouth consisting of rows and rows of tiny sharp teeth. The bloodworm had no eyes, but it smelt Pog and it turned towards him and hissed, then launched itself whip-like through the air.

Pog twirled his staff and it hit the worm with a thud. The creature was flung against the wall. It slid on to the floor, but slithered with lightning speed towards Pog as if nothing had happened. Pog raised his staff, but his attacker sprung through the air and coiled itself around it. He could feel its damp heat against his wrist.

Pog gave a deft flick with his staff so that he was holding the end furthest away from the worm. He did it with such speed the worm didn't have time to react. Pog brought his foot down on it and forced it along his staff, like a man unrolling a sock down his leg. At the same time he pulled out his sword. He held the worm in place with his foot. It was like standing on a hot, convulsing muscle. He drove his sword into the worm, impaling it on the floor. The worm spasmed once and was still.

Pog grinned.

Something coiled round his neck. He dropped his sword and staff as he felt his throat tighten and he started to choke.

A second one. Always be —

— *paying attention*, Pog thought angrily. He grabbed the coil around his neck, but the creature thrashed his eyes with its tail. Pog fell to his knees, temporarily blinded. His eyes were stinging.

He tried to suck in air, but he was wheezing for breath and it wasn't working. A third serpent-like shape slithered into view. Pog watched it helplessly as it slid past him. Meanwhile, the second one held fast. It reared above him, drool dripping from its maw.

Pog felt the coil tighten around his neck . . .

Nobody said a word as the car pulled into the driveway. Dad sat for a moment and let the engine idle. He seemed to be considering something, then he switched the engine off. Without looking at

Penny, he said quietly: 'Help your brother bring in the shopping.'

Penny watched helplessly as he got out of the car and headed for the gate. She clambered out and called after him, 'Dad? Where are you going?'

'For a walk,' he said, without turning around.

David was by her shoulder, watching. 'See what you did.'

Penny looked at him and thought about saying something, but she knew there was no point. She felt both furious and helpless. She took a bag from the car and David took another and they trudged through the front door.

Penny felt a sudden spark of fury. Why shouldn't she be allowed to ask a simple question like that? Why did she have to tiptoe around her father? She was just about to say this to David when she spotted the hall floor.

There were trails of something like wet slime criss-crossing it. The trails led from the hallway at the back of the house.

There was a crashing sound from the sitting room.

Penny and David dropped their shopping and ran towards the sitting-room door.

Even as the world started to fade, Pog was surprised

to hear his name called. He was vaguely aware of a new shadow, something by the door, then he felt something clamp itself between the worm and his neck. The worm squealed in protest.

The coils of the worm loosened. Pog gasped and air flooded his lungs. The world came back into focus.

Penny grabbing it had made the worm furious. It snapped at her face, and she ducked as she grappled with it.

Pog reached out for the worm's tail and snatched it from Penny. He pulled the head towards him, trying to ignore the smell, and Pog bit down.

Hard.

Something warm and wet splattered his face. There was a screech and the creature started to go limp. Pog clamped his jaws together even harder, ignoring the stench and mucky taste, and the feeling of warm ichor rolling between his fingers. The worm gave a final shudder and Pog unwrapped it from his neck and flung it on to the floor.

Pog stayed on his knees for a moment. Panting hard and wiping his mouth.

He heard David shout, 'Get away from her!'

He turned to see the third bloodworm wriggling up the table leg towards the urn. David grabbed the worm. The creature shrieked and whipped its head around and prepared to lunge at him.

Pog jumped, and in one fluid motion wrenched his sword from the corpse of the first bloodworm and flung it through the air.

The sword embedded itself in the bloodworm's head with a satisfyingly moist *shtuk* sound. The worm went rigid for a moment, then fell to the floor in a heap of glistening coils as David let go of its body.

The only sound in the room was the panting of Pog and two exhausted children.

They cleaned up without a word. Pog took the worm bodies outside to bury them. They scrubbed the floors and washed away the sticky black blood as quickly as they could before Dad returned. At one point, while they were kneeling on the sitting-room floor scrubbing at the stains, David reached across and grabbed Penny by the arm.

'It was going after Mum,' he said, his eyes wide.

Penny looked at him. He had never seemed so frightened and defenceless to her. She smiled and squeezed his arm.

'She's OK now.'

David nodded, then looked at the urn just to be sure.

Pog came back into the sitting room, wiping his fur. 'Bloodworms they were. Like other things from the forsaken place they eats memories. Painful ones.'

'Is that why they went for Mum's urn? It remembers.'

Pog nodded. 'Good things, but also bad.'

Penny felt sick all over again. Sick and furious, but her feelings were tempered by her concern for Pog. She thought he looked exhausted.

'Thank you, Pog,' she said.

Pog curled his lip in mock disgust. 'Thank Pog? Pog thanks David and Penny. David and Penny saved Pog's life.'

David suddenly went towards Pog and knelt down and hugged him. Pog looked surprised, but he returned the hug and patted David on the back.

Dad trailed in an hour later. They had dinner, and after a strained few minutes he was back to smiling and laughing again. Penny's anger started to fade, and the truth was she felt too tired to start any arguments. She was just relieved that they'd arrived in time to save Pog.

She lay in bed later that night, looking up at the ceiling. She strained to listen, and she was sure she could hear Pog moving around in the attic.

'Pog, is that you?' she whispered.

There came a muffled thump on the ceiling.

'I can't sleep. Can you sleep? Tap once for yes, and twice for no.'

Two thumps.

'Maybe you could count sheep. Have you ever done that? Counted sheep?'

Two thumps.

'My mum used to get me to count sheep when I couldn't sleep. It worked. Sometimes. You should try it.'

One thump.

Penny bit her lip. She was almost afraid to ask the next question.

'Pog, do you think anything else might come through the Necessary? Do you think something might get into the house?'

Two thumps.

Penny nodded then turned over to go to sleep. 'Night, Pog,' she said.

There was one more thump.

Penny closed her eyes. She tried to steady her breathing and to ignore the fact that there had been a very definite moment of hesitation before Pog had answered 'no' to her question about the Necessary and the house.

CHAPTER 19

Chumping, grumping, snuffling through the undergrowth came Bill Boggart.

Bill ploughed through the dark, on through bushes and branches, pushing them aside, tromping and trampling as he barrelled forward, snarling as he went. Moist foamy drool gathered at the corners of his rubbery lips, and he rubbed it away with his hairy forearm, giving little whimpers of pleasure because the scent was in his nose, and it was good, oh so good.

When he got to the edge of the forest he parted a bush with his great big grubby, nail-cracked, knuckle-boned hands and he spied the prize.

The house lay ahead, and inside the house were things so delicious that it made Bill's pointy, stubbly head spin with the thoughts of 'em.

'Taste good, will it, Bill?' he asked himself.

'Oh, the bestest,' Bill answered himself. 'Some proper tastlings in that there house. Bitter and tangy with pain.'

Bill stuck his slimy warty tongue out between those rubbery lips of his and made a great big wet *shluuuupping* sound in the dark.

'Ah,' he said to himself with the satisfaction of one who's supped a particularly satisfying beverage. He pulled his shoulders up and gave a little shiver of delight, and almost squealed with pleasure at the anticipation of it all.

Bill Boggart reached into the pocket of his dungarees and he took out a small, battered tin. He unscrewed the cap and sniffed the contents. He started to put some of the brown mixture on to the tip of his index finger. Then, with a delicacy that belied his humpen lumpen look, he began to draw circles, first on his forehead, then on his cheeks.

Even the comings and goings of him in the attic didn't bother him none. He was Bill Boggart. He was well used to the shadows. The darkness was his friend. Which was just as well, because Bill Boggart didn't have no friends.

And so he crouched there in the dark of the forest, and Bill Boggart hexed himself good and proper. When he was finished he knew that even his old mum wouldn't have been able to sniff him out.

Happy with his workings, Bill screwed the lid back on the tin and put it back in his pocket. He cracked his knuckles, rolled his shoulders and neck, and whispered:

'Right we be then. Let's get us some nice tastlings, shall we?'

And with that, Bill Boggart headed towards the house.

CHAPTER 20

D avid was in the forest again.

It was night, crow-black, starless and cold.

He felt a sudden warm breeze.

Help me, it whispered.

David felt the pain and anguish in that voice.

Help me.

'Where are you?' he almost sobbed.

Find me.

The darkness rippled and everything changed, and he found himself in a familiar place.

He was back in the clearing, and ahead of him was the twisted tree. It looked more contorted and in pain than ever.

This time though, he wasn't afraid. This time he walked towards it.

Even in the darkness he could see the oily slickness of the bark, like the skin of some reptile, glossy and imbued with an inner light.

David stood over the trunk.

This time he knew what he was going to see.

And this time he wasn't afraid.

The amber eye snapped open.

David sat up in bed, panting and sweating, his blanket puddled at his feet.

He took a few moments to orient himself. There was the wardrobe. There was his dresser. He was back in his room. His neck, back and chest were clammy with sweat, and the itch from the scar in the palm of his hand was ferocious. He scratched at it, enjoying the feeling of relief.

There was a breeze coming from his right.

David turned to see his new net curtain bellying outwards in a breeze. His window was open, but he couldn't remember opening it. He got out of bed and went to shut it.

He held the window frame, and for a moment he just enjoyed the breeze as it wafted in through the window. He closed his eyes.

Help me.

David opened his eyes and looked out into the

darkness where the forest waited.

He considered his next words carefully, and he knew in his heart of hearts that they were the right ones.

'I'll help you,' he said. 'I promise.'

The breeze blew the curtain in one more time.

David closed the window.

CHAPTER
21

As soon as she woke, Penny knew it was going to be one of those awful mornings. She hadn't had a morning like this since they lived in London. Back there it was always more exaggerated. The first sign was waking to a dull ache in her head, a constant throbbing that seemed to permeate everything and make her limbs feel like lead. She would lie in bed a few moments longer, willing herself to go back to sleep, knowing that such a thing was pointless.

She rolled out of bed and went to the window. It was raining outside, a steady drizzle. She could hear birdsong, a trilling warbling sound that was like a knife through the thick sodden air. The world was limbo grey. All she needed now was to hear the soft eye-watering *fsssss* of car tyres on a wet road to complete the picture.

The day continued in that grey and listless vein.

Whenever she passed David and her father they were yawning. This only made her yawn all the more, until the house was soon filled with a symphony of yawns.

Penny tried her best to read at one point, but her eyelids felt damp and heavy, and when she turned to look out the living-room window all the world was a puddled greasy smear. Looking at it just made her feel even more tired. She tried everything to keep herself awake. She was just short of pinching herself.

The rain was still sizzling down at lunchtime, and the whole world felt damp and rain-sodden.

At one point her father patted her on the shoulder to wake her because she'd fallen asleep on the chair.

She got up and moved around to try and stay awake, and she met David yawning in the hallway. That was enough for Penny – she headed straight for a comfy chair in the sitting room. The only thing that broke her torpor was what she saw there. As soon as she opened the door the urn glinted back at her, despite the dullness of the day. In all the excitement over the bloodworms' attack, Penny had forgotten how shiny the urn had looked. The sight of it made her heart quicken, and she felt suddenly revived.

She swivelled right around and headed straight upstairs. Her dad had headed for his study, and she could hear David's bedroom door close. When she reached the top of the stairs she stood right under the attic door.

'Pssst,' she said.

The attic door moved slightly, and Penny could see two tiny eyes glittering down at her through the small dark triangle.

'I meant to ask, did you clean Mum's urn, Pog?'

The two eyes disappeared, then Pog popped out of the gap he'd made and jumped down on to the floor.

Penny quickly looked behind her in case her dad should appear, and she flapped her hand at Pog.

'What are you doing? Get in there,' she hissed, pointing at her bedroom door.

Pog toddled over to the door and Penny let them both in. She shut the door quietly behind her. Pog stood looking up at her, his two paws clasped together. He looked expectant, and a little lost.

'Well, was it you?' asked Penny.

Pog nodded. ''Twas Pog. Pog did it. Was it wrong of him?'

Penny felt a sudden ache in her heart as she saw

the forlorn look on Pog's face. 'No, Pog. No. It was a lovely thing to do.' She went down on one knee before him. 'Thank you very much.'

Pog gave a small smile, but the smile quickly vanished, and he gave a furtive glance towards the window.

'What is it, Pog?'

Pog looked back towards Penny and smiled.

''Tis nothing. Nothing at all.'

CHAPTER 22

Night came quickly.

The house slept. In the attic Pog lay curled up in his den. Mouse lay nearby, his sides going in out like a tiny bellows. Dad lay sleeping too, twitching every once in a while, but fast and deep and away, as was Penny who lay serene as a statue despite the things she dreamt of. Things like terrible lonely houses in sunlight and a hot day in April. A day when she sat on a couch with David while her dad said something she couldn't quite hear because there was a roaring sound in her ears, and beneath that the sound of David crying, while two policemen stood awkwardly by the sitting-room door.

And David dreamt too. In his dream the voice called out to him and asked him for help. David twisted and turned in the bed and moaned, and he felt the night air on his limbs, and he heard the breeze whisper among the dark leaves.

Help me. Find me.

David was elsewhere. He was in the house and yet he was a world away. Too far away, perhaps.

Too far away to be ready for what was coming this night.

CHAPTER 23

Bill Boggart had decided that the boy was the most tastiest of them all.

As he made his way through the forest once again he thought back on some of the pain he'd supped in the past and how good it had been. There'd been that wood nymph who'd lost her whole family in the great fire. Her tears were so succulent that even decades later Bill still drooled to think about their sweetness and how they'd felt on his tongue. There were the lovely piquant tears of a rather stupid human who one night had got lost in the forest. Bill had realized that fear had made his tears all the more tasty, and he'd spent the night shaking branches and howling at him from the dark, rendering him senseless with the draught, and drinking in the tastiness of the man's terror when he had been sent under.

Bill patted the pouch hanging from his shoulder that contained the bottle of sleeping draught. 'Soon, my lovely,' he gurgled.

He touched the signs he'd inscribed on his forehead and cheeks, just to make sure they hadn't somehow vanished. Without them, Bill would be seen and heard and smelt like some common interloper, rather than the dashingly heroic boggart he knew himself to be. Bill's chest swelled whenever he thought of himself this way, how noble he was, how adventurous and cunning. He felt like the old, proper Bill again. No more was he reduced to pinching wood nymphs on the fringes of a marsh, or sucking pain from hibernating animals. He was Bill Boggart again, a credit to his kind, and it was all down to the arrival of the new humans in the house.

When he'd first smelt them on the air he couldn't believe it. It had been years since Bill had tasted real pain. He'd sniffed this new pain on the air, and it was thick and cloying and juicy. He hadn't come across pain like this since the First Folk had battled the creatures from the wastes beyond the Necessary.

Sometimes Bill wondered if the world would have been a whole lot better then, stained and fetid as it was, with blood and pain and the grief of others. There was real fear in the air in them days, but then Bill supposed he was just as frightened as those around him. After all, even he had to flee too, so maybe it was for the best. He could never really decide. 'Six of one, half a dozen of the other,' he would say to himself.

Oh, grief, thought Bill. *Grief which is the sweetest taste of all.* And them new humans were jam-packed with it. Like ripe juicy fruit they were, just begging to be squeezed, and Bill it was who would be happy to do the squeezing.

Bill just quivered at the thought of it. The older of the three was just aching with it. On the first night, Bill had found him in his bedroom, curled into a ball like a little defenceless animal. Bill was well hexed, so no one or nothing – especially not him in the attic – could detect him.

The girl had been next, and her pain was just as delicious. When she slept she was serene, but Bill knew that was just superficial, because beneath the surface was a writhing torrent of agony, and it seeped into her tears.

Oh, but the boy, the boy, thought Bill.

His pain was everything you could hope for.

Dark, sweet, salty, delicious. The boy was agony personified. When Bill sent him down with the draught he went somewhere deeper and more painful than the other two put together. This boy was lost in the dark, and like a fine wine in a cellar it was the dark that matured his pain and gave it such complex notes. Bill had never known pain like it. There was sorrow in it, such sweet, sweet sorrow, and there was suffering, and best of all there was rage. It was a rage that formed a delicious icing, and Bill gobbled it all up.

When he got back to the forest, he supped on all their tears and pain, but it was the boy's pain that sent him into a swirling delirium, the likes of which Bill would have been happy to experience for ever. It was a delirium that sent him a-shuddering and quaking, illuminating the inside of his head with lights of purple and gold and mauve, singing to him with a sweetness he had never known before.

Since that night Bill had returned again and again, always keeping the boy till last, knowing that to do otherwise was to risk temptation and being caught. Tonight he crept in through the back door and padded quietly up the stairs, knowing full well that he could have made as much noise as he wanted because his hex was good and strong. But still, it was no harm to be careful.

Bill went to the father's room first. The man was

dreaming and the dreams were bad. This was good, this was very good. Bill took the bottle of sleeping draught from his pouch. It was an old green bottle, mottled and opaque with age and use. Bill held it over the man's head and uncorked it. The mist fizzed softly out, and the man's nose twitched. Bill was almost bouncing up and down with the excitement. The man inhaled the draught, and Bill recorked the bottle in a hurry, for fear he might use too much of it. He watched the man's furrowed brow slacken as the sleeping draught drove him deeper, sending him a-questing for the darker, more deadly memories of his.

The man started to whimper, as did Bill when he saw the first tears glisten on his cheeks. It was the draught that brought them forth, and in his excitement Bill almost forgot his other bottle. He fumbled in his pouch for it and brought it out. This bottle was made of clear glass, and it looked like something that someone like Bill shouldn't have had on his person. It was altogether too elegant and clean-looking, but Bill knew the truth of it, and of how its glass was even more charmed than that which held the sleeping draught, and that this bottle in its own way held the greatest enchantment of all.

Bill held the top of the delicate-looking bottle to the man's face, and he watched as the tears which were coursing down his cheek started to roll towards the lip of the bottle until finally they were sucked into it. Bill corked the bottle, fighting the urge to taste, for he knew to taste meant to lose himself for a few moments, and that wouldn't do in this current situation, hexing or no hexing.

He crept out on to the landing. The girl was usually next, but tonight Bill couldn't help himself. Tonight he walked straight by her room and headed for the boy's room.

Before he turned the knob he took one last look at the girl's door. After a few moments he smiled and shook his head. Then Bill Boggart headed into David's bedroom.

And straight into the biggest disaster of his boggarty existence.

David was down in the dark. Deep down, further than he'd ever been before. The darkness echoed like a dome around him and he felt the chill wind and smelt the night air, and yet he couldn't help but shake the feeling that he was on solid ground and simultaneously floating in space.

Clear cool panic flooded his chest. He flailed and

touched nothing. He cried out and heard nothing. He was voiceless and alone. That was when he started to cry, hot tears that scalded his cheeks. His throat hurt and he felt a deep ache in his bones that he was sure would last for ever, and he knew he was lost. And then he heard the voice.

Help me. Find me.

David fought the sobs. He could feel a sharp pain cut through the palm of his right hand, and he started to concentrate on that. He clenched his jaw and focused as hard as he could. There was the voice and the pain, and he concentrated on both. Nothing else.

The voice and the pain.

Help me.

The voice and the pain.

Find me.

David answered the voice. His words were half-sob, half-scream of rage. He held on to the rage, gripped it tight like someone holding on to a piece of driftwood in a flood.

And David felt himself start to rise out of the dark.

Pog was dreaming too. He was sitting around a campfire with Grandfa and other First Folk who lived in the Burrows. Grandfa was telling them a story, and Pog was laughing so hard tears were streaming down his face.

Grandfa looked at him through the flames and smiled. *Time to wake up now*, he said.

Pog tilted his head. 'What's that now?' He heard something in the distance. It sounded like . . .

Time to wake up. Now, Pog!

A scream. Cutting through his dream like a knife.

Pog woke up. For a moment he was disorientated.

The scream came again.

It was a child's scream.

Pog bounced up and on to his feet, grabbing his sword and Grandfa's staff in the same fluid motion. He bounded straight for the attic door, shoving it aside. Beneath the child's screaming he heard a strangulated piggy squeal, a sound he hadn't heard for quite some time, but one that was all too familiar.

Pog let out a bellow of rage when he realized what had happened, and he was angry with himself for not realizing the truth sooner.

'He's hexed hisself!' he roared.

Pog ran back to his nest and quickly scrabbled through his belongings for a pouch. He found it in seconds, and squeezed it tight in his fist.

And with that Pog was through the attic door and shooting towards David's bedroom, snarling as he went.

CHAPTER 24

David sat straight up and blinked. He knew something had woken him, but he wasn't sure what.

Then he heard the gasp to his left, and he turned.

There was a short, squat dwarfish man-thing standing by his bed. It had a bald pointy head, and skin of a strange pinkish-grey pallor. It had a large mouth with rubbery lips, and only a few yellow decaying teeth at random intervals along its purplish gums. Its arms were incredibly long, longer than the rest of its body, and bristly hair protruded along its forearms. It was wearing soiled brown dungarees.

David took in all of this in a moment that seemed to go on for ever.

The strange short man-thing was clutching a clear vial to its chest in a gesture that might have been more befitting a startled Victorian lady.

'It sees us!' it squealed.

That was when David screamed. It was more a scream of rage than fear, and even as he grabbed the thing by its head and felt its repulsive cold doughy skin beneath his fingers, he still felt the rage course through him. He dug his nails into the creature's head and the thing howled.

The thing grabbed David by the arm, and an enraged, frightened David pulled its arm in return and dragged the thing on to his bed. The creature looked shocked, and was even more shocked when David started to punch it about the head.

David started to scream at it: 'Get out! Get out!'

The thing somehow managed to shake itself of its initial terror, and now it grabbed David by his forearms and snarled at him, saliva bubbling at the corners of its grotesquely large mouth. It was incredibly strong, but even so it seemed shocked at how much effort it took to force David backwards.

'You won't stop me!' David screamed, his eyes bulging, tendons quivering on his neck.

The creature tensed, and gave a great snarl—

'Grimroot!' a voice shouted, and suddenly the thing was showered with what looked like wood shavings. Except these wood shavings fizzled and sparked as they touched its skin, causing it to howl and spasm with agony. While David continued grappling with it, the creature tried to shake the pieces off. As the flakes touched it, it seemed to sharpen and become clearer, as if it had been slightly out of focus all along.

The staff hitting it in the head took it by complete surprise.

'Pog sees you now, Bill Boggart!' Pog roared, and he thrashed Bill in the temple with Grandfa's staff.

Bill flailed at him with his right hand, but this only allowed David to free his left and claw at Bill's eye. Bill howled in pain, and he tried to smack David, but Pog was too quick. Three more belts in quick succession sent him sideways, and Bill was lying on his back. Pog proceeded to pummel him about the chest and belly. Bill squealed, and he continued to flail with his huge arms, but to no avail. David was also hitting him, sometimes getting in the way of Pog's blows. His eyes were wide and wild, and he was gripped by a rage that seemed to consume every fibre of his being. He grunted and panted like a wild animal and hit out again and again ...

Bill threw himself backwards and rolled off the bed. He sprang round the corner of the bed, and loped towards the door, using his impossibly long arms to propel himself forward. He launched himself at the door, only to be hit smack in the face with a broom handle which was being wielded by Penny.

Bill skidded backwards across the bedroom floor and blinked in disbelief. Pog took the opportunity to somersault off the bed and swipe at Bill again.

This time, through luck more than anything else, Bill somehow batted Pog's staff away with his arm. He winced and howled at the pain, but he still managed to pick himself up and barrel towards the door.

He stopped for one moment, tensed himself, and then threw his head back and emitted the loudest, most foul-smelling belch anyone had ever had the misfortune to experience. It was a belch so noxious that it made everyone's eyes sting. It was so bad Penny had to fight the urge to be sick.

Bill pressed his advantage. A nauseous Penny wasn't ready this time. Bill's momentum was too much – he pressed down hard into the floor with his knuckles, his flabby pinky-grey arms tensed, and wobbled, and he launched himself skyward. Penny was only able to muster a half-hearted swipe as she brought the broomstick down. Bill smacked it out of the way, and pushed against her shoulder, using her as leverage to propel himself out into the hall. Penny was thrown forward and ended up on her knees on the floor. She managed to spring back up quickly, and without a word to each other, she, Pog, and David, all raced out of the room in pursuit of the boggart.

Pog was the quickest, shooting across the landing and launching himself at Bill, who was halfway down the stairs and already flying through the air. They collided in a clatter of limbs, tumbling over and over each other until they crashed into the front door and came to a dead stop.

Pog was first to react. He jumped up and brought his arm across Bill's neck and held him there. Bill gasped and gobbled and choked.

Penny was distracted by an object that had been thrown from Bill when Pog had collided with him. It was a bulbous bottle with a slim narrow neck, and it spun around on its side for a few moments before finally coming to rest. Penny ran downstairs and snatched it up. David was by her side, panting and sweating hard. His eyes were still wide, and he was white with rage.

'Hold still now, Bill!' Pog shouted.

Penny turned to see Pog holding Bill by the scrag of hair on his head, and with his other hand he held his sword at Bill's neck. Penny reacted instantly.

'POG! NO!' she screamed.

She could see madness in Pog's eyes. A genuine wildness that she knew was not typical of him, and she found it frightening. His eyes were dark and crazed, and she shouted at him again.

'POG!'

Pog blinked. He looked like someone just woken from a dream, and as he looked at Penny, he seemed to be recognizing her for the first time.

'Don't,' Penny pleaded.

Pog nodded at her to show he understood. He pushed Bill forward and threw him on to the ground. He sheathed his sword, and just in case Bill got any ideas, he twirled his staff and then pushed the point of it against Bill's chest.

Bill Boggart whimpered.

'Who are you?' asked Penny.

Bill pulled his head down and drew his shoulders up, like a tortoise trying to retract its head into its shell.

'B-Bill,' he stuttered.

Pog pressed the staff firmly against his chest. 'Full name and title, Bill. Manners now.'

Bill's eyes flashed with hate for a moment as they rested on Pog. Pog snarled and pressed the staff in further against his doughy flesh. The hate in Bill's eyes vanished and was replaced by fear.

'Bill Boggart,' he gasped.

Pog snarled with contempt. 'Sneaked in through the Necessary, you did. Out from beyond the forsaken place, where the trees rot and earth stinks and boggarts scratches their armpits and smells and belches all day every day.'

Penny just wanted to burst out laughing at this, but somehow she composed herself. She held up the bottle. 'What's this, Bill Boggart?'

Panic in Bill's eyes now. He stretched out his arm, and curled his fingers in and out like a child. 'Give us that. That's Bill's.'

'Is it now?' said Penny, advancing towards him. 'So what's in it?'

'Give us it, or Bill will—'

'Bill will what?' asked Penny, fury welling up in her.

Bill hissed at her.

Pog poked him with the staff. 'Tell Penny, Bill.'

'Tears,' Bill spat. 'Them's tears is all.'

'Tears?' said Penny.

Bill nodded, and then did something which gave away his true purpose. Bill licked his lips.

Penny's eyes narrowed. 'Do you like tears, Bill?'

Bill couldn't look at her now, and he whimpered.

'Whose tears are they, Bill?' Penny asked.

Bill started to shudder. The trembling started in his legs and then ran up through the rest of his body. He twisted around and shouted: 'Them's Bill's tears. Give them back!'

Penny wasn't perturbed. She bent down low to get closer to him. The rage on Bill's face started to fade, to be replaced by a look of uncertainty and fear.

'I don't think you're telling me the whole truth, are you, Bill?' she said softly.

Pog sniffed and looked down imperiously at Bill. 'They'd be your tears. Bill steals them when you's asleep. It's what boggarts do. They use the draught to send you under, so that you sleep all the more. Deep and dreaming you go while they sucks out your pain. The draught sends you away and draws your tears out.'

Pog twisted the staff even more, and Bill groaned.

'Give us it here now, Bill,' said Pog.

'What . . . what's that now?' Bill whimpered.

Pog pressed the staff down again. Bill whined. 'Draught, Bill. Give it here.'

Bill reached a trembling hand into the pouch hanging from his shoulder and took out a mottled green bottle. Pog snatched it from him, and Bill looked at it mournfully as Pog handed it to David.

'For safe keepings,' said Pog. David nodded.

'Is this true, Bill, what Pog says about the tears?' said Penny.

Bill just glared at her.

Penny stood up. She looked at the clear bottle in her hand. The glass wasn't that thick; in fact, it was a delicate little thing, and she could see moisture at the bottom of it. She felt the rage within her spill over.

Penny flung the bottle on to the floor and it smashed into hundreds of tiny shards.

'Noooooooooooo!' Bill howled, and for a moment Penny almost felt sorry for him. He tried to scrabble forward towards the remains of the bottle, but Pog held him fast. Bill leant his head against the floor, and closed his eyes and started to cry. Big tears of his own ran down his cheeks, and his hands flailed pathetically against his chest. He sobbed and snorted like a three-year-old, and Penny nodded at Pog, who prodded Bill to his feet and herded him towards the Necessary with his staff. Penny and David followed.

Pog jammed his staff against the door and it vanished in a soft fog of light, revealing the dark wasteland beyond. Bill whimpered at the sight. The night breeze which came in through the Necessary felt wonderfully cool on Penny's arms, and it was only then that she realized how hot she was. David was standing a metre or so away, still white-faced, looking at Bill with a mixture of utter revulsion and hate.

Penny stepped forward. 'Get out,' she said to Bill.

Bill looked at her, wiped a forearm under his nose and sniffled.

'Get out and don't ever come back,' said Penny.

She fixed him with a look so cold that Bill had no choice but to obey. He shambled towards the open portal. He stopped for just a moment and looked back towards the hallway, no doubt thinking of the shattered bottle of tears. This only resulted in him releasing another convulsive wail, and as he turned away Pog raised his staff to force him through the Necessary. Penny shook her head at him and Pog lowered the staff.

They watched Bill Boggart stumble into the night that lay beyond the Necessary, his shoulders going up and down like those of a sobbing toddler. Eventually he just became a grey blob melting into the darkness.

'Good riddance,' said Pog.

Pog placed his staff against the opening. The wasteland shimmered for a moment, then vanished completely as the cellar door reappeared.

'How did he get in?' asked Penny.

'Hexed hisself,' said Pog, tracing a finger over his cheeks and forehead in reference to the symbols Bill had scrawled on his face. 'Makes you disappear.'

'And he was taking our tears?' asked David.

Pog nodded solemnly. 'Tears has pain in them, the pain of memories. Boggarts like pain. They sucks it out and feasts on it. Some pain is sweeter than others, boggarts say.'

Penny thought about all of this for a moment. 'Was this why we were so tired all the time?'

Pog nodded.

'Did you know he was here?' asked David.

Pog shook his head. 'Pog only suspected. Pog smelt something a whiles back, but once you hexes yourself, all sight and smell of you is gone. Pog used grimroot to reveal him. Grimroot wipes away hexes.' Pog frowned. 'Still, though, Pog should have known and sooner.' He smacked himself on the right temple. 'Stupid Pog.'

Penny grabbed him by the wrist. 'Pog's not stupid at all. Never say that.'

Pog looked at her.

Penny raised her eyebrows at him. 'I mean that, Pog.'

David looked panicked now. 'I saw him – before you threw that grim root stuff at him, I *saw* him.'

He looked from Penny to Pog and back again, as if searching for an answer. Pog frowned for a moment, then shrugged. 'Bad hex, maybe. A big fool is that Bill Boggart. Probably hexed hisself all wrong.'

David nodded, but he didn't seem convinced. He was still very pale, and Penny could see the trace of wildness in his eyes.

'Dad!' she suddenly shouted.

They all looked towards the stairs, half expecting Dad to appear.

'He must have heard it all,' said David.

Pog chuckled. 'No. No. Not a thing heard by him.' He motioned them to follow him.

They all trooped upstairs and Pog led them into Dad's room. Penny was hesitant at first, but in she finally went, and when they were in the room the first thing she was struck by was the sense of peace.

Dad was lying in bed facing the ceiling. His blanket was pulled right up to his neck as if someone had just tucked him in.

Pog hit the floor with his staff, and he started to

shout: 'Wooo oooo! Wooo oooo!' Before Penny and David had time to react, he leapt up on to the bed and shouted in Dad's face, 'Woooo ooooo! Woooo ooo! Wakey wakey, Dadling.'

Penny and David were stepping forwards to stop him, but Pog just held out his paw.

Their dad hadn't moved. He hadn't even twitched.

'Sleeping draught,' said Pog. 'Sends you deep down.' Pog tapped one of his own ears. 'You can't hear. Wears off, but you sleeps so deep, and then having tears taken makes you . . .' Pog shook his head.

'It makes you feel exhausted. That's why we've been feeling the way we have,' said Penny.

Pog leapt off the bed. 'That's what does it,' he said.

Penny felt helpless and angry all at the same time.

'We should have killed him,' said David.

Penny whipped around and glared at him. 'David.'

'Still, we should have,' said David, but this time he said it with a look of guilt on his face. That look gave Penny some measure of relief.

For some reason, for the next few seconds they all just stood there and looked at Dad. The only sound in the room was his breathing. Until finally Pog spoke up, sounding a little surprised by himself:

'Pog is hungry.'

CHAPTER 25

Pog liked pancakes.

For some reason, Penny found this to be the most startling revelation of all since they'd first met him.

She and David sat at the kitchen table, while they watched Pog wolf down a stack of them.

'Fightings gets Pog all hungry,' said Pog, through a mouthful of pancake. He smiled at them, and Penny smiled back. David was sitting beside her, and he was just picking at a pancake with his fork, his eyes wide and staring into space.

'Will he be back?' asked Penny.

Pog licked and smacked his lips and swallowed down a lump of pancake and shook his head.

'Bill Boggart won't be back. His magicks won't work here no more. Defeating boggarts sends 'em away. Catch a boggart and they loses their power. He can come here no longer. House is bane for him now – Bill Boggart can step over the threshold of the Necessary no more.'

Pog shovelled more pancake into his mouth and raised his eyebrows and looked at Penny as he munched.

'So he came through the Necessary and made himself invisible.' said Penny.

Pog nodded. 'Hexed hisself with a strong hex so Pog couldn't hear or smells him passing through. Then Bill hid in the forest.' Pog narrowed his eyes. 'There a long whiles he was, Pog reckons.'

Penny frowned. 'These things coming through, are there more of them than before? I mean, there were the worm things. Has there been anything else recently?'

Pog swallowed and gave a quick shake of his head, but Penny noticed him lower his eyes.

'Pog will patrol,' he said, turning towards the window. 'Just in cases.' He turned back to Penny. 'Something was up. Nothing's up now. But Pog will patrol anyways.'

Penny smiled. 'Thank you, Pog.'

Pog shrugged.

Penny turned to David. 'Are you all right?'

David gave her a surly defensive look. "Course I am.'

Penny didn't press the matter. David looked even more exhausted than ever. There were dark circles under his eyes, and they were round, huge and haunted-looking.

'We should all get some sleep,' said Penny.

'Fine,' said David, leaving his seat at the table and exiting the kitchen.

Penny looked at Pog across the table. 'David's very tired.'

Pog nodded, and he seemed to consider saying something, then maybe thinking better of it, he returned to his pancakes.

CHAPTER 26

David waited until he was sure they were all asleep. He sat on the edge of his bed and heard Penny come up the stairs. He listened out for Pog climbing back up into the attic, and when he heard the door being pulled across he held his breath and waited a little longer.

Time passed.

When he was sure he couldn't hear another sound, he put his clothes on. He dragged his boots out from under the bed and put on his jacket. He never thought to look at his watch, but he knew it was sometime between night and dawn, a time when a stillness lies over everything, and the world is ghost-like and muffled.

David picked up his torch, then went quietly out of the house and walked into the night.

He smelt it before seeing it. The forest seemed particularly pungent and mossy in the dark, as if his nose was making up for what his eyes couldn't see. David switched his torch on, and flinched as the beam lit up the trees that stood before him. He almost expected them to flinch too, as if he had come upon them unexpectedly and surprised them as they conversed secretly in the dark.

Nothing moved in the beam of light. Nothing stirred on the air.

David stood dead still and held his breath.

Then he plunged into the darkness.

The forest passed him by in what seemed like moments, and he found himself in the clearing. A chink of light from the moon escaped over the lip of a passing cloud and lit up the twisted tree. For some reason David thought it would be indecent to keep the torch on. He switched it off and found that it was bright enough to see by the light of the moon.

David wasn't frightened. He only had one thought in his mind. The one thought that had been on his mind since he had screamed it in his dream just before being attacked by Bill Boggart.

I will help you. I will find you.

David closed his eyes and clamped his lips tight as he heard those words again.

'You came,' a voice whispered.

David opened his eyes and wheeled around to see who had spoken.

The figure was standing on a low branch of the tree, silhouetted against the night.

The creature was even shorter than Pog. It was pointy and skinny, its arms held out by its sides, as if it was about to leap away. One thing was obvious from the start: it was made of bark and wood. Its amber eyes were set in a dark wooden face. Twigs streamed back from its head like fronds caught in floodwater. These twigs were an approximation of something that looked like human hair. There were tiny flowers sprinkled throughout the twigs. Its nose was pointed and crooked, like a crone's or a witch's nose. Its chin was pointed and curved upwards, almost meeting the nose, and its bark-like skin was wrinkled. Its fingers were long and simul-taneously delicate and clawed. It had large feet with pointed heels, and it spoke with a man's voice, but with a soft, gentle quality.

'You came,' it said again.

'Yes,' said David, not knowing what else to say.

'You freed me,' it said, with a tone of childlike wonder.

David nodded. The creature's head dipped and

tilted like a bird's as it regarded him. Its amber eyes narrowed.

David stepped tentatively towards the tree.

'Who are you?' the bark creature whispered.

'I . . . I'm David. David Cresswell. Who are you?'

The creature hunched up its shoulders and rubbed its spindly fingers together, and there was a slight creaking sound as it smiled at him.

'I am Kipwik. Kipwik Sterndel.'

There was a pause.

'Pleased to meet you, Kipwik Sterndel.' David surprised himself by stepping forward and holding out his hand.

Kipwik looked at it. He waved his head slowly back and forth, then he looked from David's hand to his face and back again. He reached out, and placed his right hand in David's. David was surprised. It was like holding a tree branch, but one that was warm and alive, as if blood circulated beneath the bark.

Dark blood, he thought. *Dark, yet warm.*

For some reason his vision seemed to cloud. He shook his head, then pumped his hand gently up and down. Kipwik looked curiously at their hands, then looked back at David's face. David took his hand back.

'You freed me from the tree. You sundered me from my prison. How can I repay you?' said Kipwik.

David's mouth opened, but no words came out. Eventually he just managed to stutter: 'I–I don't . . . I don't know . . . I'm not . . .'

Kipwik crossed his ankles and spread his arms out wide and bowed. 'No matter. You may decide how I can repay you later. For now, I am grateful.'

David looked at the tree. 'How did you end up in there?'

Kipwik sighed. 'It is a long and unpleasant tale, best saved for later.'

'I haven't told anyone what happened. I haven't told them about you,' said David, knowing somehow that Kipwik would want to keep this a secret. He wanted to gain his trust. Somehow he knew that was important. He scratched the scar on his palm. 'I promise I won't tell anyone,' said David.

Yes, it's the right thing to do, he thought.

Kipwik nodded. 'I am very grateful. There are those who would seek to do me harm, and I am weak and vulnerable after my incarceration.'

David looked back at Kipwik and swallowed twice. 'I heard you. You called to me,' he blurted. He swallowed again in an effort to calm himself. For some reason he could feel a hotness in his eyes, and the familiar ache in his throat that meant he was near tears.

Kipwik just tilted his head and gave him a curious look. Eventually he nodded. 'You came. Yes you did, David Cresswell.' Kipwik slowly shook his head. 'But it was not I who called you.'

On hearing those words, David felt something snap inside himself, and he started to cry. He cried so hard that he fell to his knees before the tree and leant his forehead against it. He sobbed and he sobbed, and as he wept Kipwik gave him another curious look. He reached out a hand, and he laid it gently on David's head. Without looking up, David grabbed Kipwik's hand with both of his and held it there.

A cloud moved over the moon.

The darkness covered the corpses that lay out of sight behind Kipwik's tree. It covered the hare with its broken neck. The fox that had been torn and gutted. The many squirrels that now gazed sightlessly into the night.

And the darkness covered Kipwik's face.

CHAPTER 27

Penny woke later that night to the sound of heavy rain thrumming against the roof and windows. For a moment she wasn't sure where she was. The sound of the rain seemed to be everywhere.

She raised her head from her pillow as she remembered that something else had woken her. She got out of bed and opened her bedroom door.

David was standing outside his own bedroom and was just about to go in.

'David? What are you doing?'

He turned to her. He was soaked through, but it didn't seem to bother him. He had a strange faraway look on his face, as if trying to focus on what was in front of him required a bit more effort than he was willing to use.

'Just . . . nothing . . . I thought I heard something outside. I wondered if it was that boggart thing coming back.'

Penny tilted her head. 'Pog said he couldn't come back.'

David nodded, and looked towards his door. 'Right, yeah.'

Penny frowned. 'You should get dry.'

'OK then, night,' said David, without looking in her direction. He went into his room.

Penny thought for a moment about knocking on his door, just to ask him again if he was OK, but she was tired, and the steady rumbling of the rain was loud and soporific. She went back to bed and she was asleep within moments.

And so they all slept, lulled by the steady drumming of the rain: a steady *thrum thrum* that brought a deluge down upon the forest, the likes of which it hadn't seen for an age. The rain ran through the roots of trees, and beat down the heads of flowers; it hit with the kind of force that bounced branches up and down, sometimes to breaking point, and soon the forest floor became littered with broken branches and twigs.

Rivulets of water gathered and coalesced and ran between the trees and softened the earth until it became a gloopy runny mess, and it was this water that raced in torrents down the steeper inclines of the forest.

For a while there was only the sound of the rain.

Then, as if something had been stirred from its slumber, a wind began to rise. It became stronger with each passing moment. The rain had stripped some of the leaves from the trees, and now these wet leaves rose up and they began to spin around and around, spinning with increasing intensity, until very soon they revolved with the fury of whirling blades.

The trees seemed to creak and bend beneath the weight of something more dreadful than the rain, and the whole forest seemed to groan as if a great and ancient wheel, long since rusted and dormant, was beginning to turn again. The wind started to howl, and a tremor ran through the forest as lightning split the night sky.

Something was coming.

Something dark.

Something terrible.

PART
4

A Collision
of Worlds

CHAPTER 28

David told no one about Kipwik, and he constantly thought about going back to see him. There was something about him, something terribly old and wise in those amber eyes of his, and David suspected that he might be able to help him.

He was still haunted by the voice in his dreams. But now there was something more. Now there was something in the dark of those dreams. Something that glowed in the distance. It looked like a face, white with a black mouth. Screaming.

It was for this reason that he found himself back in the forest clearing a few days later.

It was early evening, and the tree and everything around it was a ghostly grey this time. David looked around. It didn't seem as threatening as it did at night, but in its greyness and solitude it still felt cut off from the rest of the world.

He walked further into the clearing, twigs snapping under his feet.

'You'd best be careful, sweetling. Some of them used to be my brothers.'

David heard a light chuckle on the breeze and his head snapped around in an attempt to locate where it had come from. He could feel the hairs prickling on his neck.

'Over here,' said the voice.

David turned back to the tree. There was a smaller felled tree beside it, and Kipwik was sitting on it, one leg crossed over the other. His hands were clasping a raised knee. He smiled.

'Closer, sweetling. I don't bite.'

David steeled himself as he walked towards Kipwik. He stopped at what he thought might be a safe distance.

Kipwik grinned at him. His face creaked slightly, and the wind rustled the tiny leaves in his twiggy hair. His skin looked less dry, healthier. There was an ease to his movements that he didn't have before.

'You look different,' said David.

'I am. I'm stronger now that I am free.' Kipwik breathed in deeply through his nose and closed his eyes. 'Stronger. More connected.' He opened his eyes and smiled. 'You came back.'

'Yes,' said David. His throat felt dry, and his voice came out as a croak.

'Why?'

David looked at Kipwik for a moment, then he looked at the ground. 'To see if you were all right,' he said, after a long pause.

Kipwik unclasped his knee and spread his arms wide. 'And here I am, fit as a fiddle, and all thanks to you.' Kipwik crooked a finger at him. 'Come. Come closer.'

David swallowed nervously, but he did as he was asked. Kipwik's eyes shone, and the closer he got, the more David marvelled at their lustre and deep colour. They were alive and vibrant, and they glowed with an amber light that made him wonder what they looked like in bright sunlight. *Eyes filled with wisdom*, he thought. *Eyes that know the answers.*

David was only inches from Kipwik now, but even so, he found his nervousness was starting to diminish. He could see the bark that covered Kipwik. It was dark and leathery, but it shone like healthy skin. His face was wrinkled, particularly at the corners of his mouth.

Because he smiles lots, thought David. *And can*

anyone really be all bad if they smile a lot?

He rubbed his forehead. The first thought had been his, but the second one felt strange and invasive, as if it belonged to somebody else. David blinked and shook his head. It felt like he'd just walked into a cobweb. He started to scratch the palm of his right hand.

Kipwik tilted his head, and frowned in concern. 'What ails you, young one?'

David shook his head. 'Nothing.'

Kipwik leant back and raised an eyebrow.

David hadn't noticed them before — he'd been too distracted. But there they were. Two eyebrows. Two ridges patterned and shaped by delicate grey-green leaves. He noticed the way the breeze made the tiny purple flowers in Kipwik's hair tremble. He smelt something like pipe smoke. It was strangely reassuring.

He cleared his throat. 'Nothing really.'

Kipwik gave a wry grin. 'Nothing really is the liar's way of saying, "something definitely".' He raised both eyebrows now and looked right at David.

David found that he couldn't meet his eyes, and he turned his face away. 'How did you end up in that tree?' he asked, his voice slightly high-pitched as he tried to sound relaxed. He looked at the border of the clearing, and he heard the rasp of wood on wood as Kipwik moved nearer to him. David surprised himself by turning back and not feeling afraid.

Kipwik was sitting close to him now, and he too was looking at the trees. He narrowed his eyes and pursed his lips, and David could see the lines of age around his mouth.

'This forest was a bad place long long ago.'

Kipwik said nothing further for a moment. He just looked straight ahead. David felt a light breeze on his neck and he shivered.

Then Kipwik looked up at him, and his face was stern now. 'There were monsters here, sweetling. Horrible creatures. Vile. Foul. They believed that because they were here first, the world belonged to them. They hid themselves away from your kind, creeping around, hidden by arcane magicks, the sneaky snivelling little rats.' Kipwik's face scrunched up as if he was about to snarl or spit. 'The place was infested with them, and they didn't take too kindly to me.'

'What did they do?' David asked. He swallowed nervously.

Kipwik sighed as he gazed upon his former

prison. When he looked at David again his face was filled with pain. 'One of their elders magicked me into the tree. Kipwik born of tree, now exiled within the body of one for all eternity. That a life should come full circle in such a horrid way. That an imp as noble as I should be imprisoned for wanting the best for the forest and its more genteel inhabitants. Thinking on it, young David' – at this point Kipwik's voice became choked – 'thinking on it makes me weep with sorrow for what was lost.'

Kipwik bowed his head, and very soon his shoulders went up and down as he sobbed. David wasn't sure how to react, but he felt sympathy for his friend. He reached out and touched his shoulder, and without looking up Kipwik rested a hand on his. Once again David was surprised by how warm it felt.

When Kipwik looked up, David saw tears of amber on his wooden cheeks. Kipwik tried to smile.

'But you're here now, dear David.'

David smiled in response, and he felt himself swell with a certain pride. He felt stronger all of a sudden, as the feeling surged within him. And yet there it was again, that sensation that he was experiencing something that was outside himself.

Kipwik wiped away his tears delicately with the tip of his index finger. 'Remember your promise. You must tell no one that I am here. There are still monsters. There will always be monsters. And some would seek to destroy me once and for all if they knew I had escaped.'

David squeezed Kipwik's hands. 'I promise. I've already seen one of these monsters.'

'You have?' Kipwik gasped.

David nodded. He told Kipwik quickly about Bill Boggart. He told him how Pog had helped him and Penny banish Bill.

'That was very good of your friend,' said Kipwik, 'very good indeed. But I fear that one slip of the tongue, one word spoken in error, might be heard by the wrong ears. With monsters about one must always be careful.'

David looked around him. The trees swayed in the breeze, and he felt a new chill.

'Can you feel it, David?'

David nodded. 'Yes.'

'Since the storm. Something is rising. The wheel is turning. I fear a most dreadful age is already upon us.'

Neither of them said anything for a moment, then a look of concern passed over Kipwik's face.

He stood up and placed a gentle hand on David's shoulder.

David rubbed his hands together, and he found he couldn't look Kipwik in the eye again.

'What is it, David?'

David looked at the ground . . .

'When I said . . . when I said nothing was wrong . . . not really. Well, what I should have said . . .'

David swallowed.

'My mum died,' he said hoarsely.

There were images in his head. Images he didn't want to see, but they presented themselves anyway.

'Go on,' said Kipwik, ever so gently.

'Me and Penny, we were home from school one day. I remember the sun was . . .' His last few words were angry. He almost spat them out.

Kipwik nodded in understanding.

'I was in my room and Dad called me. I went downstairs and he was in the sitting room.' David swallowed hard, and he gasped as if it was hard to breathe. 'There were two policemen there, and Penny was on the couch and she was crying . . .'

David was looking past the twigs and branches and grass, past the very earth itself.

'They didn't even have to say anything. Mum

had gone to the shops in the car and there'd been an accident, and . . .' David shook his head and squeezed his eyes shut. 'I knew before I came down the stairs, I knew . . .'

David said nothing for a moment. He remembered the strange hush that had settled over the house as he came down the stairs that afternoon. The sensation of a terrible weight pulling him down.

'They said a truck had . . . a truck had spun out of control . . . and she . . .'

A stricken-looking Kipwik squeezed his shoulder.

'And I keep hearing the voice,' David sobbed. 'I hear it in my dreams, and sometimes I think I can see a face.'

David could see it now – a gauzy white phosphorescence in the dark, away in the distance. Sometimes he even fancied it had a mouth, a blackness torn and twisted into that luminous gauze, and he knew it was calling him. He knew it was in pain.

Help me. Find me.

David turned to Kipwik. He could barely see him through his tears.

'I thought the voice was you, but it wasn't. I think I know who it is now. I think I know who's been calling me.'

Kipwik held his breath for a moment. Then he sighed and closed his eyes.

'A voice like that, dear David – a voice heard in the dark is very often one who is close to the listener.'

David shifted position.

Kipwik shook his head in awe. 'In fact, quite often it is one who has been lost. One who has left this world and is trying to get back.'

David felt his heart leap. His hand went to his chest, and Kipwik smiled warmly at him.

'It's my mum, isn't it?' David buried his face in his hands and wept.

Kipwik looked near tears himself. He patted David on the back. His voice was soft and low like the breeze. 'Shhh, sweetling. Shhh. All will be well.'

Eventually David wiped the tears from his eyes and sat back on the tree trunk. 'Sorry,' he said.

'For what?' asked Kipwik.

'For crying. For being such a baby.'

Kipwik gave a sad smile and shook his head. 'Weeping for those we have lost is the most natural thing in the world.'

There was silence for a few moments before David spoke again. 'Why was I brought here?'

Kipwik frowned. 'The forest called to you. It

brought you here to rescue me because it sensed the good in you.'

David didn't look convinced. 'But the voice. I keep hearing it. I thought it was calling me here, but even though I helped you I can still hear it. I can still see her—'

He couldn't finish the sentence. He pursed his lips and his nostrils flared as he tried to contain the emotion welling within him.

'*Help me. Find me.* That's what she keeps saying.' He turned on Kipwik. 'What does it mean? Where is she? She's calling to me, isn't she? Where is she?'

Kipwik looked guilty, and he turned away from David and walked along the trunk of the tree and stopped about a metre away as if in contemplation.

'What does it mean?' David begged him.

Kipwik let out a deep sigh, and he raised his face up to the sky and closed his eyes. 'Oh, David. Dear David.'

The wound in David's palm was itching, and he scratched it.

'Your mother has gone from this world, and that is the way of things. All things must perish and go.'

'I know,' said David. 'She died. I know.'

Kipwik came back towards him and laid a hand on his forearm. His breath was sweet as flowers, and

David could smell that pipe-smoke scent again. Something about it calmed him.

'When we finally leave this world we go elsewhere.'

Kipwik suddenly looked perturbed. David could feel a panic rising within him.

'What? What is it?' he demanded.

Kipwik took in a breath. 'There are worlds other than this. Worlds that are just a heartbeat away, and worlds that are infinities distant from ours, worlds indeed only a step away, and sometimes in our passing . . .'

David looked at Kipwik. He took in every crack and line and leaf, he saw every pore on his face. He willed him to finish.

'. . . sometimes in our passing some can get trapped somewhere we were not meant to go.'

David let this sink in for a moment. The feeling of panic started to flutter again in his chest.

'Where . . . where is she?'

Kipwik tried to look him in the eye, but he turned his face away.

David thought about the wasteland he'd seen beyond the Necessary. He thought about the dreams he'd had, and the smell of dead things being carried on the air. It was just like the smell that had come through the open doorway. He started to tremble.

'It's somewhere bad, isn't it? She'll be in danger,' said David.

Kipwik nodded, and his eyes were filled with pity and sorrow.

'I think I know where she is,' David said. He grabbed Kipwik's arm. 'She wants me to find her. She wants to me to look for her.'

Kipwik regarded him for a moment. 'Yes,' he said.

'Then I can find her. I can bring her back. I can do that, can't I? If people go elsewhere, then they can come back. If she's trapped somewhere, because that's all it is, she's not dead, is she? That's what she's been trying to tell me! She's just trapped!'

David's voice was ragged. He was still gripping Kipwik's arm. Kipwik looked in his eyes as if searching for something.

'Sometimes, in passing over, people do get trapped,' he said.

David held his breath.

'And sometimes . . .'

David could feel pressure build in his chest, in his ears, until it became a roaring sound.

'. . . sometimes they can be rescued.'

*

They spoke for what seemed a very long time, and the more they spoke, the more hopeful David became.

Kipwik told David he would guide him, and that under no circumstances was he to tell anybody about the quest they were about to embark upon. It would put them all in danger, he said, and there was no sense in imperilling those he loved.

He then told David of his plan. It frightened David, but Kipwik saw the look on his face and reassured him that it would work.

David felt relief wash over him. He thanked Kipwik over and over as Kipwik smiled patiently. When David asked him again if he was certain it would work the 'yes' Kipwik uttered made his heart leap with joy.

And so it was decided. They would enact the plan immediately.

'Time is of the essence,' Kipwik said, smiling encouragingly.

They left the clearing together. The light was still grey, but David felt it was infused with a brightness and a luminescence it hadn't had before. *That's hope*, he said to himself.

Hope.

The forest started to darken, but that didn't bother David.

He only thought about the light.

CHAPTER 29

'Nothing's up,' Pog said to himself. 'All is well.'

This is what Pog told himself, even though he was starting to patrol in wider circles each night. Even though he went deeper and darker into the forest. Even though the forest seemed quieter and no animals stirred. No badgers snuffled in the undergrowth, and no foxes cried out in the dark. Even though Bill Boggart had been banished and he knew he had no reason to patrol.

But still there was that niggling feeling.

Had something else passed through from the Necessary?

'No,' Pog said to himself. 'Not possible.'

He was pottering around in the attic when he heard Grandfa's voice: *Well, Pog?*

Pog looked up into the darkness. He tilted his

head and narrowed one eye. 'What?' said Pog. 'What's to do now?'

There was no reply, of course, and Pog felt slightly guilty for speaking with a hint of insolence. He sighed again and turned back to his nest.

Did you pay attention, Pog?

Pog turned back and squinted up into the darkness. 'What's that?'

Silence for a moment. Then the voice again. *Did Pog pay attention?*

Pog shuffled awkwardly from one foot to the other. 'Course he had. 'Course he'd been paying attention. He was Keeper of the Necessary. But despite his unwavering self-belief there was a tiny doubt. 'Pay attention to what now?' he asked.

There was no answer. Pog twirled around and around as he looked up towards the ceiling.

'What's to do now?' he demanded.

Pay attention, that's what's to do, Pog. Go ask the world.

Pog stood there and crossed his own arms and sniffed. Pog was doing his duty, and all things were well.

And yet . . .

He'd missed Bill Boggart, but that was understandable. The hex Bill had used was strong. Bill was

221

banished now, and surely that was the end of it.

But he was still patrolling, and hadn't he been going further each night? Why was that now? And since when had he started?

Pog looked at Mouse, and Mouse looked at Pog.

Without thinking he went into his nest and grabbed Grandfa's staff. He strapped it to his back, sheathed his sword, then up he climbed, until he was on one of the rafters looking down at Mouse.

'Pog has to do something, Mouse.'

Mouse didn't seem too bothered, but Pog nodded at him anyway, and up he went and slipped out through the roof and into the night.

It was warm and dark, and he could smell grass on the breeze. Pog took in a deep satisfied breath, then he slid down the roof, grabbed a drainpipe, and slithered down quick and silent as you like.

Away out the gate he went and along the road. Bats circled above him, and something white and swift and silent flew past him at one point. An owl, no doubt, but Pog didn't tarry to check. He had only one thing on his mind.

He scurried into the forest, and he didn't stop until he felt something give ever so slightly in his chest. It was like a click, or the snap of a twig, like moving from cold to inner warmth. It was like fording a river and knowing your legs were just the right strength for the current, and all you had to do was hold your concentration right here and now and you would be across to the other side in no time.

Here, right here, thought Pog. *Right here seems to be best. Ask the world. See what it says.*

The wind rattled the leaves, and he heard the low creak of branches. Pog looked around him and saw the perfect candidate and walked towards it.

The oak tree was old, and its trunk was the broadest thing Pog had ever seen. Pog knelt by it and he placed one hand on a root, and the other in the warm wet soil beside it. Pog closed his eyes. Pog did as Grandfa had once taught him all those years ago. Pog *pushed*.

Pog listened.

Pog asked the world how things were.

The tree spoke to him, the roots spoke to him, the soil spoke to him: Pog and the earth were as one. He felt his mind's eye rush back through the darkness, rush back through time. He felt a jolt and a quick shudder as he realized he had gone far, far back. He saw the Necessary open, lightning forking inside it, shadows gathering within it, ready to infect the world. There was a gust of wind and he felt the sting and slap of poisoned earth and foul air. He saw the Burrows, the soft rolling mounds of grass and earth that were people's homes. Figures walking among the mounds, oblivious to the oncoming threat. Pog felt like screaming at them. Then he was overwhelmed by a sudden vision of flame as the Burrows started to burn.

Pog pulled back from it, and he urged his mind on forward. There were distant screams, and Pog felt the tears come to his eyes. They were hot and scalding, but he tried to ignore them, and instead he listened to the world, this world, the green world – and gradually, slowly, the stinging sensation dissipated, the stench left his nostrils, and he found he was breathing pure air where once there had just been rot and filth, and there were birds singing, sunlight flashing, the world bubbling like a stream as it went on its way, and something . . .

No, he thought.

Something had changed.

Something had shifted slightly, and now the world was different, and for a brief horrifying moment he smelt the stench of rotten meat again.

Pog gasped and his eyes flew open. 'No!' he shouted. 'Stupid Pog. Stupid stupidest Pog!' he roared.

The storm was nothing. Something had

happened before then. It had happened not long after the Cresswells had arrived.

Something broke through the brush to his left, and Pog whipped out his staff. 'Who's that now?'

The figure was grey and wraith-like in the gloom.

'Pog?' it said.

'David,' Pog replied, exhaling with relief.

'I was out for a walk,' David said.

Pog looked at him. The boy looked thinner. His eyes were dark and lined, and there was a glittering in them that Pog recognized as the fire of someone who was pushing themselves to the brink of exhaustion. Pog felt a terrible pity for him. He wanted to go to him, to tell him that all would be all right. But that would be a lie, wouldn't it? Especially now. Especially after what the world had told him.

David's eyes darted from side to side, as if he was struggling with something.

'Pog . . .' he said.

'Yes?' said Pog.

There was a silence as David took his hands in and out of his jeans pockets and shuffled from one foot to the other. He looked lost.

'Pog, do you think . . . do you think it's possible to talk to someone . . . someone who's gone?'

Pog nodded in understanding. The boy was talking about his mother.

'Yes. Pog talks to Grandfa. All things be possible.'

David nodded and bit his upper lip. 'But when
that person is gone . . . I mean, really . . .'

David turned his head away. When he turned
back, tears were welling in his eyes and his voice
was hoarse. 'If you knew you could get Grandfa
back, what would you do?'

Pog felt tears prickle his own eyes now, but he
straightened up and looked fiercely at David. 'Pog
would do anything. Pog would move the world.'

David nodded in gratitude and clamped his hand
over his mouth. Pog smiled encouragingly, but
David shook his head and let out a sob.

'I'm sorry, Pog.'

Pog frowned. 'Sorry? What fo—'

A root, blackened and twisted, whipped out from
under the soil and wrapped itself around Pog's
ankle. Pog was thrown off balance, but he reached
for his sword, only for another root to unfurl from
the forest floor and knock the sword from his hand
and wrap itself around his wrist. Pog was pulled off
his feet and the air whooshed out of him as he hit
the ground.

He could see a dark figure crouched behind

David, its clawed hands dug into the soil as it poisoned the earth and commanded it to do its bidding. Two more roots broke through the soil and curled tight around Pog's other leg. More still erupted and laced themselves around Pog's chest. Pog fought, but the roots just held him tighter and tighter. As he struggled he tried to focus on the shadowy figure, but it was deep in darkness, a gnarled silhouette with amber eyes, trembling as it moved the roots against him.

Couldn't be, Pog thought. *Not possible.*

Pog hissed, 'Villain! Murderer!'

The shadow gave a low cackle. Pog felt as if his veins were filled with ice. He strained against his bonds, but he couldn't move. Roots moved languidly across him like snakes.

David stood over him and reached down and picked up Pog's staff.

'Well done, young David. Well done,' whispered the shadowy figure.

Pog glared upwards, willing David to look at him. David's tear-filled eyes flicked over him briefly, and then he turned away in shame. He was murmuring something over and over again to himself agitatedly, like someone lost in a night terror:

'I had to, I had to . . .'

Pog turned to see David and the spindly shadow leave. David gave him one last distraught look before disappearing into the trees.

CHAPTER 30

The house was quiet, not even giving vent to its usual creaks and moans, as if it were waiting for something.

The front door opened, and David entered carrying the staff. Kipwik sidled around the door and rubbed his hands together.

David felt dazed, as if he'd been punched. He could still see the look in Pog's eyes, and he swallowed hard, fighting the urge to be sick.

Is this the right thing to do? he wondered.

This was followed immediately by a second thought that brought with it a buzzing sensation, as if a bee was trapped inside his skull.

Of course it is, sweetling.

David rubbed his eyes. The buzzing sensation faded.

'First things first, David,' Kipwik whispered. 'We must make sure not to be disturbed.'

David nodded. He headed to the kitchen where he'd hidden Bill Boggart's bottle of sleeping draught according to Pog's instructions. The bottle was buried far back under the kitchen sink beneath a pile of rags. David looked at it. Kipwik had told him it was needed: 'It will ensure we are not disturbed when the door opens.'

'But what about Penny?' David had asked.

Kipwik had gently touched his forearm and smiled. 'It will be safer for her and your father this way.'

David had nodded, suddenly seeing the sense in it.

David went up the stairs, pausing at the top step. He looked down at Kipwik.

Kipwik gave him an encouraging smile and waved him on. 'Go on, David. It must be done. They must sleep to ensure that we are not disturbed. I will go to the portal and meet you there.'

David held the staff out. 'Do you want to take the staff?'

Kipwik smiled and shook his head. 'No, no, you must keep it. It is your responsibility. Your quest.'

David nodded. He took a deep breath and headed towards the back of the landing. He would start with Dad. His legs felt leaden, and there was a gnawing inside himself that he tried to ignore.

It's for the best, he thought. *We can't risk being interrupted. Then once this is over and we're—*

He didn't dare complete the thought. He didn't want to hope too much for fear he might be disappointed, but it was enough to harden his resolve.

He made his way to his father's room and crept in. He felt strange, as if he was somehow separate from the rest of the world, as if he were wearing one of those old Victorian deep-sea diving suits. He laid the staff on the floor.

He stood over his sleeping father, and he uncorked the bottle.

He was too busy looking at the vapour seeping out of the bottle to pay attention. He didn't see his father's eyes flicker behind his lids, and he wasn't prepared when his father's hand suddenly jerked upwards and knocked the bottle from his hand.

David tried to grab the bottle, but it squeezed between both his hands and landed on the blanket. More vapour escaped, and David's heart pounded in his chest. He saw his father's face twitch and slacken. He was almost smiling. David held his breath. There was no movement from his father, and he was snoring slightly. David picked up the bottle, while being careful to clamp a hand over his mouth and nose. He shook it. It was empty.

He picked the staff up and made his way back to the landing and stood for a moment, paralysed with guilt and terror. Kipwik was nowhere to be seen.

David looked at Penny's bedroom. Without the draught there was no hope of making sure she slept through the next few minutes. He would just have to hope the portal opened quickly and that it would be too late for her to stop them. Afterwards, she'd understand why he had to do it.

The four of them would be together again.

CHAPTER 31

'Stupid Pog. Should have known,' Pog hissed.

He struggled against his bonds. Without Kipwik's influence they were inert, but they were still fixed fast.

'Stupid,' Pog said again, tears of frustration rolling down his cheeks.

He pushed again.

A tiny shadow suddenly darted into the space just outside his field of vision. There was a soft thump, and something landed on his chest and thrust its face into his.

'Mouse!' Pog shouted. 'You followed Pog!'

Mouse raised himself up on his hind legs and squeaked as loud as he could, his head moving back and forth.

Pog heard them before he saw them. The patter

of dozens of feet on earth. The bobbing silhouettes that slipped through the gaps in the trees. 'Squirrels!' he cried, laughing so hard tears sprang to his eyes.

Squirrels hopped up on to the roots binding him, squeaking to each other. A stocky shape waddled into view, snuffling and chittering. It was a badger, and she was followed by three others. Along with the squirrels and Mouse they set to work gnawing at the roots. The roots had been diseased by Kipwik's touch, so they made swift work of them. Pog pulled himself up and out of the remains of the roots and picked up his sword. He bowed before the badgers and the squirrels.

'Pog thanks you from the bottom of his heart.' He bent down and patted Mouse on the head. 'And Pog thanks you most of all, Mouse. But Mouse must stay here now. Pog has something dangerous to do.'

Pog stood up and smiled at his rescuers, then he turned and started to run.

CHAPTER 32

Kipwik was by the cellar door as promised when David made his way back downstairs. He was busy studying it, his long fingers working gleefully together.

'They sleep deeply, yes?'

David nodded.

Kipwik smiled. 'Well done, David. So very well done.'

David stepped forward and thrust the staff towards him. He wanted to get rid of it as soon as possible, as if surrendering it might absolve him of his betrayal of Pog.

Kipwik's face twitched and he shook his head vigorously. 'No, no, *you* must wield it.' David frowned. Kipwik licked his lips and took half a step back, keeping his eyes on the staff.

'What's wrong? Why won't you touch it?'

Kipwik's lips trembled, and his amber eyes filled with tears. 'Dear, dear David. I simply can't.'

'Why can't you?'

Kipwik shook his head. Tears streamed down his face.

'Please take it,' David begged.

He thrust the staff towards Kipwik. Kipwik's eyes widened, and he screamed as the staff touched him and a sudden gout of green flame erupted from his chest.

David dropped the staff and started beating at the flames on Kipwik's chest as he rolled around on the floor. 'I'm sorry, I'm sorry!' he wailed.

The flames were extinguished, and Kipwik lay trembling on the floor, his chest going in and out as he gasped and wept.

'I'm sorry,' said David once more, holding his friend by the head, rocking him back and forth.

Kipwik pushed him gently away and looked up at him and smiled. The smile became a wince as he held a hand to his chest. 'I forgive you, David. You weren't to know.'

'Know what?'

Kipwik pointed at the staff. 'This abomination is the work of those monsters I told you about.'

David's stomach lurched. 'What? I don't under-stand.'

'The one who wielded it was the one who banished me into the tree. He was an evil sort, Lumpkin-born. He went by the name of Lemuel. He was the grandparent of your little friend. Fancied himself as a sage, a wise man, but like all First Folk he was a monster at heart.'

David felt as if the world was tilting. 'Pog . . . Pog is his grandson?'

Kipwik shook his head sorrowfully. 'Like many of his kind your friend was misguided. What you haven't been told is that I and those like me sought refuge in this world long ago. Our land was blighted by a terrible evil, and yet the First Folk would not allow us passage.' Kipwik looked at David with pity. 'Sometimes a mere matter of perspective is all that separates us from the monsters.'

David thought about the bloodworms. His head felt fuzzy. He thought about the worm heading for his mum's urn. 'But . . . but . . .'

And now there was a sound, as if something was screeching in the distance. He heard something like claws scraping at wood. He looked at the door of the Necessary. The cracks around it seemed to be widening. The door itself almost looked as if it were bulging. David took a step back.

Kipwik touched him on the arm. 'We must hurry, David. Your mother. Think of your mother.'

An image entered David's head. A torn blackness in white gauze, screaming in the dark. David felt a sudden surge of anger and terror. He stood up with the staff in his hands.

Kipwik urged him on. 'Now, David. Now is the time.'

David looked at the Necessary, and he felt the warm wood between his hands. He held the staff parallel with the floor. As Kipwik smiled, David remembered what Pog had done and he took a deep breath.

'David, what are you doing?'

Both David and Kipwik turned to see Penny at the end of the hallway.

David smiled, and tears sprang to his eyes. 'Pen. I'm going to bring Mum back.'

Penny looked stunned. 'David? Whatever it is you're doing, please stop.'

David wiped a hand across his eyes, and he gave a manic, desperate grin. 'I'm opening the Necessary, Pen. Mum's trapped on the other side. I've seen her.'

'Mum's gone, David. Mum's dead.'

David felt an iciness squeeze his heart. 'No,' he moaned.

Kipwik showed his palms in a gesture of supplication. 'Don't listen to her, David. Her mind has been turned by the Lumpkin.'

'I don't know who or what you are,' Penny snarled, 'but you need to step away from my brother.'

Kipwik grabbed David's hand and squeezed. David felt a wave of nausea so strong that it almost made him retch. He heard the voice.

Help me. Save me.

'Listen to her, David. Listen to your mother,' Kipwik whispered.

'She's gone!' Penny shouted.

Kipwik squealed, his squeals quickly becoming snarls as Penny walked towards them. 'No closer!' he roared.

'Murderer!'

The shout came from behind Penny. She stood aside to reveal Pog standing behind her.

'Kipwik Sterndel!' Pog roared. 'Fiend! Murderer!'

Kipwik gave a bow and a flourish with his hand. 'At your service. So nice to meet another Lumpkin after all these years.'

Pog growled.

'The last I met was your grandfather – Lemuel. A fine fellow indeed. He imprisoned me in a tree with this very staff, which is why I can't touch it. What's that term you First Folk are so fond of using?'

'Baned,' Pog hissed.

Kipwik nodded. 'But I have my friend David to help me now. Isn't that right, David?'

David was weeping quietly. Every part of him felt heavy.

Kipwik's face twitched. 'David?'

David started to shake his head. 'I don't know . . . I don't know . . .' He could hear the wretched cries behind the door, the thud of slithering coils against wood. Kipwik touched his hand lightly and David straightened up and squeezed the staff.

'You's hexed him!' Pog snarled.

'What did you do to my brother?' demanded a furious Penny.

'A light blood hexing, nothing more. Just enough for a bit of gentle persuasion.' Kipwik smiled, but his eyes were filled with malice.

''Tis how he saw Bill Boggart,' Pog said.

Kipwik shrugged. 'An irrelevant side effect.'

'Who are you? What do you want?' Penny asked.

'The great evil,' spat Pog. 'Him who came

through the Necessary before. Him who along with others destroyed the Burrows as First Folk tried to defend this world.'

Kipwik wagged a finger at him. 'And don't forget he who delivered the mortal blow to your beloved grandfather. I saw him as he locked me into that tree. Such a pity I never got to see him stumble away, bleeding in the night, to finally fall and lie still. His bones consumed by the earth that you First Folk profess to love so much.'

Pog roared and stepped forward brandishing his sword, but Penny grabbed his shoulder.

'No, Pog.'

Kipwik had raised his hand. A vicious-looking thorn was sprouting from his palm. He raised the thorn over David's hand. David looked at it. It seemed vague and distant to him, like everything else that was going on around him now.

'Listen to her, Lumpkin,' he snarled at Pog. 'I can deliver a full hexing. He'll burn from the inside out from blood fever.'

'What do you want?' Penny asked.

Kipwik looked at her with mock pity. 'What I've always wanted, sweetling. To suck the juices out of this world the same way I sucked the other world dry.'

'You mean the world on the other side of the Necessary?' said Penny.

Kipwik grinned.

'That's what they's do,' said Pog, his hand twisting around the hilt of his sword. 'They moves from place to place, eating memories, eating pain, sucking life from things, till nothing's left but husks and bones, and then they moves on.'

Kipwik spread his arms wide. 'This world is so full of light and the forces that bind things together. And pain too. So much of it. Lovely delicious pain. Enough to sate my appetites, and others.' He ran a tongue along his lower lip and grinned at them.

David watched him, as if he were far away from his own body. He shook his head. 'No,' he said.

Kipwik flinched. 'What?'

'I won't. I can't,' said David. The sound behind the door was reaching a shrieking crescendo.

Kipwik's eyes widened with panic. He looked from David to the staff, then he looked at Pog and Penny. Slowly he smiled and shook his head as if indulging the mood of a spoilt child. 'No matter.' He placed his hands gently over David's hands as they gripped the staff, then he drove it into the door.

David heard a scream, and a blinding whiteness filled the world.

CHAPTER 33

To Penny, it felt as if a hurricane had popped out of nowhere and knocked her and Pog off their feet. This wasn't like the previous opening of the Necessary. This was a violent tumult of noise and light.

Penny struggled to sit up. Pog was on all fours staring straight ahead. He was emitting a primal howl of grief. Penny couldn't see exactly what was going on. The light was still flaring, but as it started to dissipate she saw what Pog's eyes were focusing on.

Grandfa's staff lay in glowing splinters on the floor. Kipwik was prancing before the remains, and David was on his knees, staring in shocked disbelief at the fragments.

The Necessary was also gone, and in its place was

a gaping maw in the wall through which a stinking wind howled.

Kipwik stood with his head held back, the wind streaming through his hair, his arms outstretched.

'David!' Penny called.

David didn't seem to hear her. He was slouched, still staring at the staff fragments.

'The key. The key be broken,' Pog sobbed.

Penny felt as if the whole world was lurching under her feet. 'Can we lock it again?' she shouted over the wind.

A stricken-looking Pog shook his head. He started to pant furiously as he eyed Kipwik. He stood up and drew his sword and started towards the imp.

A shrill chittering from the Necessary made him stop in his tracks. Penny heard it too, and she frowned.

They scrabbled around the edge of the door, skittering across the walls and floor, a few at first, then more, until there were dozens of them coming in waves.

'Greebeldies!' snarled Pog.

Penny looked at him, her curiosity about his use of the familiar word forgotten as the first of several greebeldies smacked into him.

Pog slashed at them with his sword, dispatching three of them within seconds, skewering two more together.

Penny looked around desperately for something to fight with. She could only kick out at them with her slippered feet, hitting one straight in the face with a satisfying smack, stopping it mid-squeal. She grabbed another by one of its legs and flung it against a wall. Pog thrust his sword through another, pinning it to the floor before it could launch itself at her.

The horrid screeching made them both turn.

There were dozens upon dozens of bloodworms pouring through the gap between the two worlds. They slithered together in a black mass, mixing with the gnashing greebeldies. The floor and walls were roiling.

Penny looked despairingly through the hubbub of snapping pincers, writhing coils and shrieking mouths to see David still kneeling on the floor before Kipwik. She made to step forward, but a panting Pog grabbed her arm.

'Too many for now. Must retreat and gather ourselves.'

A reluctant Penny tore herself away, and she and Pog headed for the hallway.

'We need to close the Necessary. How can we do it?' Penny shouted.

Pog looked at her, half-panicked, half-enraged. 'Can't be done.'

'Pog?'

Pog raced to the sitting-room door and held it open for Penny. Penny saw his eyes widen, and she slipped sideways just in time to avoid a greebeldy which had launched itself at her.

Pog drove his sword upwards, and the greebeldy shrieked and convulsed in agony. Pog whipped his sword sideways and the greebeldy's corpse flew out across the hallway.

Pog grinned at Penny as he turned back towards the sitting room. 'Pog is—'

An enormous bloodworm landed on his back. It whipped around him with such speed that Pog was hurled against a wall. The diving head of the bloodworm drove itself downwards into his face with the force of a punch. Pog dropped his sword and he crumpled to the floor. The bloodworm was about to plunge its teeth into him but Penny grabbed it by the tail and flung it with all her might.

The bloodworm was too surprised to react and it was sent tumbling across the floor. Penny grabbed Pog by the lapels and started to drag him into the sitting room. She could see the bloodworm righting itself and wriggling frantically towards her. She grappled with the doorknob, threw the door open, dragged Pog in and slammed the door shut just as the bloodworm hurled itself against it.

She laid Pog gently on the floor, ignoring the thudding and shrieking on the other side of the door.

'Pog!' she shouted, cradling his head.

There was no response. Pog's head lolled alarmingly, and Penny stroked his cheek.

'Pog,' she sobbed.

Her hands and arms were shaking, and she kept calling Pog's name, but he was still, his breathing shallow.

CHAPTER 34

David turned his head to look out into the wasteland. Greebeldies and bloodworms were still flooding in, and along the horizon he could see dark shapes, coming slowly but surely across the dead earth.

Kipwik's hands were clasped together as he looked through the Necessary. His amber eyes were shining with tears of joy.

'Look at them, David. Look at them. Once we sate ourselves on the pain of this world we will turn it into a husk,' he said hoarsely.

'What did you do to me?' David moaned. He felt so suddenly cold and empty after the Necessary opened, as if something had been ripped out of him.

Kipwik stood before him, pity in his eyes, and he

stroked David's cheek. 'I'm sorry, David. I've released you from the blood hexing. The visions and voices it presented you with were falsehoods, simple lies and conjurations. But know this, I am forever grateful.'

David looked at the shattered pieces of the staff on the floor. A few greebeldies were chewing on the shards, wisps of light fizzing gently upwards from the remains. Other greebeldies sniffed in the ethereal vapour, eyes rolling in their heads. David thought he was going to be sick.

Kipwik had turned his attention back to the Necessary, and David lowered his head.

'I'm sorry, Pog,' he whispered huskily.

CHAPTER 35

Penny stroked Pog's face, but there was still no response from him. She could hear the scrabbling and moist chittering outside the sitting-room door. There was a delirious bubbling sound, as if the greebeldies were expressing their collective delight, while the vile hissing of the bloodworms provided an even darker note.

She thought of David out there, broken and alone. She clenched her fists and then wiped her eyes and stood up.

'I'll be back, Pog. I promise.'

Penny faced the door and gathered herself for a moment. Then she opened it.

The hallway was filled with greebeldies and bloodworms swarming over each other, gnawing at the stairs, the walls. They seemed to be extracting a gentle white vapour from everything. She could see the door of her dad's study was ajar. The glowing vapour was stronger there, and the sight of it made her tremble with rage.

In her mind's eye she pictured David still slumped on the floor. Penny picked up Pog's sword.

A greebeldy turned from gnawing at a banister and looked at her and frowned. Penny glared at it and raised the weapon.

The greebeldy snarled. Two more of its companions followed suit.

Then they rushed her.

CHAPTER 36

Pog was standing in a meadow. He looked at the green world around him, at the leaves made golden with sunlight, at the sky which was a flawless powder-blue. He closed his eyes and he felt the warmth of the sun on his face. Pog smiled.

'What's to do now, Pog?'

Pog turned in the direction the voice had come from.

Grandfa was sitting on a tree stump no more than a metre away from him, smoking his pipe.

For just a moment the world swam before a dizzy Pog.

'Grandfa!' he gasped.

Pog ran to him, stopping just short for a moment, as if afraid he might cross some forbidden barrier. The corner of Grandfa's eyes crinkled, and his brown eyes sparkled.

'Well then?' he said.

'What now?' said Pog.

'Answer Grandfa's question. What's to do?'

A sudden wave of sorrow hit Pog. 'Pog has failed, Grandfa. The Necessary is open. Things have passed through.'

Grandfa shrugged. 'Pog must close it so.'

Tears sprung to Pog's eyes. 'But Grandfa's staff is broken.'

Grandfa squinted up into the blue of the sky. He took a couple of sucks on his pipe, then he held it out and pointed it at Pog. 'What did Grandfa's staff do?' he asked.

'Locked the Necessary,' said Pog.

Grandfa raised his eyebrows and shook his head. 'Just that?'

Pog frowned. Grandfa kept smiling. The sight of it warmed Pog like a glowing ember that kept getting hotter and hotter . . .

'It remembers!' he shouted.

Grandfa nodded. 'The monsters seek the pain that soaks into the world. The pain of memories, of things lost. They hunger for it. But pain is not what kept the Necessary closed, and pain is not the everything. Pain mingled with its opposite is what makes us who we be. Take one and you take from the other and you diminish what people be, tall folk and First Folk alike.' Grandfa puffed on his pipe. 'Pain and its opposite,' he mused. 'Both are powerful, and one cannot exist without the other.'

For Pog it was like the final piece of a puzzle clicking into place. He knew now what had been happening. Ever since the Cresswells had moved into the house the creatures beyond the Necessary had sensed their grief and sought to feast on it. The Necessary itself had even started to weaken. The staff had no longer been enough to keep it locked. Now there was nothing powerful enough to close it. And yet . . .

'There be something the monsters cannot fatten themselves on,' Pog said. 'Something besides pain. Something more powerful!'

It came to Pog as he remembered all the times he'd looked at the staff, and all the times he'd remembered, not just the things lost but the times shared, the moments that gave him strength. Fishing with Grandfa. Stories by the fire. The bliss of sunny days, and the feel of Grandfa's paw in his. The moments that were made all the sweeter and more precious because of that pain. Now he finally understood that there was something else to cling to despite all the sadness.

'Joy!' he shouted.

Grandfa smiled broadly. 'What's to do now, Pog?'

Pog clenched a fist. 'Close the Necessary. That's what's to do.'

Grandfa nodded in appreciation.

Pog grinned, but his throat felt raw, and he could feel tears again. 'Is this you, Grandfa? Is this real?'

Grandfa just looked at him for a moment, then he shook his head and gave a sad smile.

Pog's shoulders slumped.

Grandfa tapped the side of his own head. 'But Grandfa is here.' He tapped a hand just over his heart. 'And here.'

Pog smiled, but the world was swimming through his tears.

Grandfa was beginning to fade. 'Go now, Pog,' he said, his voice a whisper on the breeze. 'Rise up.'

Pog woke up on the sitting-room floor. He felt a lump on his head. It stung slightly.

He closed his eyes and gathered his strength for a moment, then he sensed something like an unseen presence and he opened them again.

Pog felt his strength flow back into him, just as the fierce whiteness that glowed behind him started to illuminate the room.

CHAPTER 37

Penny stabbed with the sword and it connected with the first greebeldy, lopping off one of its forelegs with an ease that surprised her but that surprised the bug-eyed greebeldy even more. It hit the floor and started to spin around shrieking as it tried to scrabble away.

Penny plunged the weapon deep into its back. The greebeldy spasmed. Penny didn't have time to check to see if it was dead because she was already pulling the sword out and aiming it at another greebeldy. She sent that one hurtling across the floor, but a larger one had already launched itself through the air, and there wasn't enough space between them for her to react in time. Its pincers snapped in and out, its eyes crazed. Penny could only brace herself for impact.

There was a sudden orange-golden blur and the greebeldy disappeared as it was snatched out of the air by a lunging fox.

Penny looked on in disbelief. The fox had the greebeldy between its jaws. It bit down hard and shook the shrieking thing until it was limp, then it flung it to the side and leapt at another greebeldy.

For a second Penny was too stunned to move. Another fox leapt into the fray, and Penny had to blink when she saw what she thought was a badger ripping out the innards of a bloodworm it had felled in the centre of the hallway.

She turned to see a sudden flood of squirrels coming through the front door. More badgers followed, and they were joined by a storm of birds, owls, blackbirds and crows. The wave of animals and birds fell on the stunned greebeldies and blood-worms and the whole hallway became a hurricane of feathers and teeth and howls and screams.

Penny managed to collect herself and she plunged into the fray, striking vile creatures left right and centre, howling for joy herself as she saw them pecked by crows, bitten by badgers, ripped by foxes.

Joyous, angry, Penny fought her way back to the hallway where David was still on his knees at the end.

'David!'

He turned to look at her, his face pale and tear-streaked. Kipwik was about a metre away from him, gazing adoringly into the wasteland. Fewer monsters were coming through the opening between worlds, but Penny could feel a strange kind of pressure in her head, as if a storm was approaching, and she could faintly hear a distant howling. Things seemed to be getting gloomier. There was a smell on the air, brackish and swamp-like.

Penny dispatched two bloodworms, cutting through them with ferocity as she made her way to David. Birds were diving at a group of panicked greebeldies and she saw some foxes tear a blood-worm in two between them, but there seemed to be a no-go area closer to the Necessary that only the monsters themselves would cross.

Penny pushed on, and she felt the pressure of something push her back, but she lowered her head and forged forward until she was only a few metres from David.

Kipwik stood beside her brother and placed a hand on his shoulder. He grinned at Penny. 'Do you feel that?' he said, eyeing her maliciously. 'That force coming from what your friend used to call the Necessary. More of my children are coming.'

'Get away from my brother,' Penny snarled.

Kipwik waved a finger at her. 'You didn't say please.'

'What do you want?' Penny shouted.

Kipwik smiled patronizingly. 'Everything. We consume all, devour all. All those energies that bind you to each other, your lovely memories, your emotions.' He laid a hand on the wooden floor and a patch of it blackened at his touch, as if it had become infected and rotten. 'We take your pain. Without the hard carapace of suffering, you have no protection. We hollow you out. We leave the world a husk, devoid of all its energies and defences. Your world is ours now.'

Penny brandished the sword. 'Not if I can help it.'

Kipwik displayed his palm. The thorn was still sprouting from it, and he held it over David's head.

'Coward,' said Penny, feeling a shiver of delight as she saw the flicker of rage in Kipwik's eyes when she said the word.

'You can't stop me, little one.'

A voice rang out over the sounds of struggle in the hallway. 'Maybe if Penny was alone, imp. But Pog is here now!'

Penny's heart quickened as she turned to see Pog standing behind her. He had the urn clasped under one arm. Something small and brown scampered across the hallway, ran up Pog's leg, across his chest and into the breast pocket of his jacket.

Pog grinned. 'Correction – Pog and Mouse.'

Without even thinking, Penny tossed his sword to him. Pog caught it and winked at her.

'First Folk filth!' Kipwik shrieked. 'Go back to your scattered people. Tell them what's to come.'

Pog's grin was ferocious. A greebeldy flung itself at him, but Pog barely looked as he gave a deft flick with his wrist and the greebeldy hit the floor in two parts. Pog sheathed his sword and stepped towards Penny. He held out the urn and smiled up at her.

'It remembers,' he said.

Penny took the urn. She looked at it, felt the weight of it, the subtle lines that ran along it. She held it to her chest and she nodded at Pog.

The urn began to glow with a fierce golden-white light. She could see images in the light. Flickering ghosts of times past. Times spent with David, with Dad.

With Mum.

Penny turned towards Kipwik. Kipwik lowered his head like a hunted animal, his hand still poised over David's head.

'What's that? What's it doing?'

Penny shrugged. 'Do you have family? I mean, proper family? Do you remember them?'

Kipwik took half a step back, then forward again, snarling.

'This remembers, like Pog's and Grandfa's staff. Memories are like magic, I think – they make things powerful. That's probably why your monsters eat the painful ones, but that's all they can do, just devour them and they're gone. The First Folk knew better, I think. They knew there were memories your kind couldn't stomach.' She looked at the urn, her eyes glittering. 'Like layers, Pog said. All those memories and emotions laid down. I think, like the staff, a thing like this can become something more, because something else gives it a power.'

'Joy.' Pog grinned.

Kipwik started to shake his head.

'I think we have something that you can't fight,' Penny smiled.

Kipwik lunged at her as the urn blazed with a white hotness. He made it halfway across the space between them, but something stopped his momentum – David had grabbed him by the ankle.

Two shrieking greebeldies scampered towards David. David kicked one away, while Pog's sword flew through the air and took the other in its soft underbelly.

Kipwik managed to scramble free, and he hurtled towards Penny.

Penny didn't know why, but she just laid the urn gently on the ground.

Kipwik was upon it, his eyes shining with rage and madness. He reached out for it.

A wave of light shot out from the urn – *WHOOMF* – and hit him full force. Kipwik spun backwards, arms and legs flying, tumbling over himself.

David had pulled Pog's sword from the greebeldy's corpse, and now he slid across the floor towards Pog, who snatched it up.

Penny heard Pog snarl, and she turned to see a torrent of greebeldies and bloodworms behind them, scrambling over each other as they tried to get to their master's aid.

Pog didn't hesitate. He ran forward and met them head-on, spinning and stabbing, bobbing and weaving through the air, while the birds and the beasts plunged into the mass of creatures and gnashed and tore at them, holding them at bay.

Penny turned back to see Kipwik make another attempt to reach the urn. She felt a strange calm descend upon her, and somehow she knew she didn't have to move.

The pressure on her shoulders came as a surprise – the sense of hands holding her in place, warm and protective. She felt a familiar presence, and she smiled.

WHOOMF. Another wave of light hit Kipwik and he squealed as he flew backwards again.

Dark, snake-like shapes were feeling their way around the edges of the door. Kipwik pointed at them and laughed as he tried to get back on his feet. 'Look! They come! More of my children. Whatever *that* is' – he sneered at the urn – 'it won't work.'

Penny felt the hands squeeze her shoulders. She thought she heard a whisper. A familiar voice she hadn't heard in some time. Tears sprang to her eyes. She enjoyed the look of fear and confusion on Kipwik's face as she smiled at him.

'These are things you can never touch,' she said. 'These are memories more powerful than you can imagine.'

Another wave of light from the urn reached the edges of the door. The tentacles recoiled, and there was a huge collective shriek.

Kipwik screamed. He turned this way and that in his fury, and his eyes lit on David. He turned on him.

Penny saw David pick a piece of wood off the floor, saw him raise it up over his head. It was a fragment of Pog's shattered staff. David drove it downwards into Kipwik's eye.

Kipwik's scream mingled with the screams of the creatures from beyond the portal. He stumbled around, clutching his eye, green flame spewing from the blazing socket and between his fingers.

Penny went to David and grabbed him. She felt Kipwik's clawed hand clutch at her sleeve.

Penny kicked him away with all her strength, straight through the doorway that had been the Necessary. The light from the urn blazed bright, and both David and Penny were thrown off their feet as one final wave of light rushed towards the opening. There was a roar and then a long, hot silence that covered everything.

Penny wasn't sure how long she'd been lying on the floor. She raised herself up on her elbow and blinked her eyes rapidly in an attempt to banish the brightness. A panting David was kneeling across from her. He looked exhausted. Two squirrels came up to him and looked at him inquisitively. A badger toddled forward and helped push Pog into a sitting position. It licked the palm of his hand, and a dazed-looking Pog glanced over at Penny. They both turned towards the wall.

The opening to the other world was gone, as were the cracks. There was nothing there now but a plain old wooden door.

'The Necessary is gone,' said Pog, sighing with relief and lowering his head to his chest.

Penny went to David and helped him stand. They both stared at the wall.

'I'm sorry, Pen. I'm really sorry,' he said.

Penny shushed him. 'You couldn't help it.' She put her arm around him and Pog came and stood with them as they gazed upon the new door.

A sudden impulse gripped Penny, and she reached her hand out towards the doorknob.

'Pen?' said David nervously.

Penny looked at Pog. He smiled at her.

She turned the knob.

The door opened.

There was no wasteland, no greebeldies, no bloodworms – just some stairs that led down into the cool darkness of a gloomy cellar.

'Where have the monsters gone?' asked Penny.

'Sealed back in the forsaken place,' said Pog. 'All which don't belong have been magicked back there.'

Penny looked down the hallway to see a river of squirrels leaving through the front door. There were foxes scattered in among them, and the birds were leaving too. The badger was by Pog's side.

'Thank you,' said Penny to the badger. It nodded and waddled away, following its friends back to the forest.

'Animals suffered too. The imp Sterndel killed them for sport,' said Pog. 'They fought to preserve their home and to avenge fallen comrades.' He turned back to look at the doorway and shook his head in awe. 'Closed for ever,' he whispered.

Mouse squeaked in his pocket and Pog smiled down at him.

Penny was still supporting David. She felt Pog's paw in her hand, and they stood there a while, not quite believing what had happened. They might have stayed like that in silence if Penny hadn't suddenly remembered something a bit more pressing.

'Dad!' she shouted.

PART
5

Pog in the Light

CHAPTER 38

Dad woke up a day later. He arrived into the kitchen, tousle-haired and giving a great stretchy yawn as David and Penny sat at the table eating their cereal.

'So, what have you two been up to?' he asked, his back turned to them as he searched the cupboards.

Penny smirked at David. 'We've been adventuring, Dad.'

'Saving the world.' David grinned.

'But we cleaned up afterwards,' said Penny, winking at David. She was grateful for the fact that the shabbiness of the house meant that any damage inflicted in the battle would most likely go unnoticed by their father.

Their dad sat with them and started to shake his cereal out into a bowl. He spoke to them but concentrated on his breakfast. 'That's nice.'

Penny and David were holding their giggles in.

Their dad started munching on his cornflakes, looking out over their heads. 'I suppose you were hanging out with Pog,' he said.

There was a stunned silence as a gobsmacked Penny and David first looked at each other, then at their oblivious father who kept munching away, his eyes fixed on a point on the opposite wall.

'What? Who, Dad?' Penny eventually managed to splutter.

'Pog,' said her dad matter-of-factly. 'Your mum's imaginary friend.' He looked into his bowl and moved his spoon around.

Penny looked at David, who could only shrug in disbelief. 'What do you mean?' she asked.

Her father looked at her. 'Your mum had an imaginary friend when she stayed here with your great-grandparents. She called him Pog. Apparently she used to drive them crazy with her stories about how he was here to guard some mystic portal or something, and that he fought monsters.'

'Why would you only mention that now?' Penny asked sharply.

Her dad frowned. 'What do you mean? I only just remembered. It was a silly thing, but she liked to talk about it. She claims he helped her find her way back when she got lost in the forest.' He shrugged. 'I suppose lots of people have had imaginary friends at one time or another.'

David looked at Penny, his mouth opening and closing as if he wanted to speak but could no longer form words.

Penny shook her head and smiled and looked at the table. She suddenly had an idea, something pure and simple, one so obvious that she couldn't believe she hadn't thought of it before now. But then she supposed it wasn't something easily done. She looked at her father.

'Dad? I think we should do something. Something important.'

She told him her idea. For a moment he looked a little nervous, almost frightened. She could sense David's anxiety also as he sat ramrod-straight in his chair, but he too began to relax as he listened to what she said.

'What do you think?' Penny said.

Dad's smile was faltering, a little sad. 'We could do that,' he said quietly.

Penny grinned, and she reached across the table and squeezed his hand. 'We could,' she said. 'It'd be nice.'

He nodded then started to rise from his chair, shaking his head. 'It's the funniest thing. I feel as if I've been asleep for days.'

It was two days later when Penny looked out of her bedroom window and knew that today was the day. The sky was blue and the sun was shining, and a light breeze was riffling through the trees. She met David coming from his bedroom, and he nodded to signal that he was ready.

Dad was a trickier affair. He pottered around for a bit, coming up with various excuses for not going outside. Penny packed her bag in the sitting room with David's help. That was when they heard the whisper.

'Pssst. Here now.'

They turned to see Pog standing with a rucksack on his back.

He looked at them a little guiltily. 'Pog has to go away.'

Penny felt a quick sinking sensation.

Pog must have noticed because he added: 'But not for long. Pog can visit. Pog just has something to do.'

'What is it you have to do?' asked Penny, knowing full well what the answer would be.

'Pog must find his people. As Keeper of the Necessary, Pog was bound here by his promise, but no longer. The Necessary is gone. World is sealed tight for ever.' He gave a faltering smile. 'Pog can go home now. Through the forest Pog must go,' said Pog, taking the moment to look and point at the window, but really to avoid looking in Penny's eyes.

Penny was already hugging him before he had a chance to turn around. David followed suit.

'I'm sorry, Pog,' said David.

'So David said already,' Pog said. '''Twasn't David's fault.'

'Sorry, Penny,' said David, looking over Pog's shoulder.

'It wasn't you, David,' said Penny. 'It was Kipwik.'

David nodded, still keeping a tight hold of Pog.

'Pog is very grateful, but Pog can't breathe.'

David let him go and they all stood looking at each other for a moment.

'So,' said David, wiping his eyes.

'So,' smiled Penny.

'So,' said Pog, his eyes shining.

Pog cleared his throat and shouldered his bag. 'What will Penny and David do now?' he asked.

'Penny and David' – Penny chuckled – 'have something important to do.'

Pog nodded. 'Pog will return.'

'I don't doubt it,' said Penny. 'Just one thing, Pog.'

Pog tilted his head.

'There was a little girl who used to live here. You told her about greebeldies and things, didn't you?'

Pog nodded.

'What was she like?'

Pog smiled. 'Brave. Brave and true. Just like Penny and David.'

They said their goodbyes and Penny felt a strange mixture of sadness and happiness. Pog went out through the window while Penny and David went to meet their father in the hallway.

Their father was clean-shaven for the first time in what seemed like ages. He seemed a lot less nervy and apologetic around them than he had been. He looked more like himself, Penny thought.

'We ready then?' he asked.

They all made their way out the gate and headed for the forest. It was a warm day. The air was clear, the sun bright. It felt like one of those days when everything had found a perfect balance. Everything was just right, from the warmth of the breeze to the scents of the flowers. They chatted amiably as they made their way into the depths of the forest. Penny felt a new feeling. A sense of wholeness she hadn't experienced since her mother had been alive.

She thought of her mother now, and she remembered the whispering presence she'd felt just before the Necessary had closed. It was warm and comforting, and sometimes when she was alone now she still felt that same presence, and it made her feel as if she could accomplish anything.

It didn't take them long to reach somewhere they all felt comfortable with. There was a green hollow in the forest, a place of peace. The only sound was the breeze in the trees, and the occasional birdsong.

'Right then,' said Dad.

Penny felt her heart do a little leap, and she exchanged a quick glance with David. She took the bag from her back and gently lifted out the urn.

Penny's dad looked at her and David and nodded.

Penny unscrewed the lid of the urn. The wind took the fine light-grey cloud of ashes, and they all watched in silence as they floated out into the forest, into the green and sunlight.

'Them that's dead is never gone,' Penny whispered to herself, and it was as if just saying the words themselves gave her strength. She looked up to the sky and closed her eyes and felt the sun on her face.

She felt her father's hand in hers, then David's.

'Thank you, Pog,' she whispered.

Pog watched the Cresswells from a distance. He saw them hold hands, then they all turned together and left that place, and he felt a strange tugging sensation around his heart.

As he walked on, Pog thought about how he'd felt when Penny had hugged him, all fierce and proud as if he might burst with both sadness and happiness. Part of him wanted to stay with the Cresswells, but another part of him knew his destiny lay elsewhere for now.

Pog stopped suddenly.

He looked at the vista that lay before him. He was facing a meadow not unlike the one he'd seen in his vision of Grandfa.

Pog looked at the meadow bathed in sunlight. He realized this was the furthest he'd ever been from home. Grandfa had brought him fishing and foraging in many places, but never this far. Never to a place like this. This was new and far away, and Pog felt himself on the brink of something. He laid a gentle hand on his breast pocket where Mouse lay sleeping.

He looked at the line of shadow on the ground that separated him from the meadow. He looked up at the great deep-green and cool canopy of trees which towered over him. He steeled himself, then he asked a question:

'What's to do now, Grandfa?'

The branches of the trees waved lazily in the breeze.

Just one more thing, Pog.

'What's that now?' said Pog, his eyes now brimming with tears of his own, because he knew full well what the answer would be.

Time to say goodbye, Pog.

Pog nodded. He tried to be as brave as he could, but he had to lower his eyes to the ground. 'Goodbye so, Grandfa,' he said.

Good Pog. Brave Pog. The bravest. Grandfa loves him more than the world.

When Pog looked up again, there was nothing but the gentle hissing of the wind. *Nothing else to do now, Pog, but one thing*, he thought to himself. *That's right*, he said to himself, *dry them tears*.

He looked out across the meadow drenched in sunlight. For a moment he thought about asking the world how things were. *No need there either*, he said to himself. All was good. He smelt the air and admired the trees, and all was green and bright and fresh.

And then he spied movement ahead in the trees across the meadow. Small figures, waiting for him. Far away and faint, but he saw them beckon to him, and Pog knew who they were and his heart leapt.

Are you alone? the little girl had asked him.

Pog shook his head and smiled.

'What's to do now, Pog?' he asked himself.

Only one thing to do now, he thought.

Pog stepped into the light.

ACKNOWLEDGEMENTS

A big thank you once again to the brilliant Chicken House crew. Thank you Rachel Hickman, Rachel Leyshon, Jazz, Esther, Sarah and the brilliant Elinor Bagenal for all your help this year. Thanks also to Laura Smythe for her support. Thank you, Laura Myers and Sue Cook for knocking the final manuscript into shape. A big, big thank you to Barry Cunningham for applying his wisdom to *Pog* when it was needed most. An extra special mention for my brilliant editor Kesia Lupo for being so clear-eyed and assured when I couldn't be, and of course most importantly for championing Mouse.

My thanks also to Jane Newland and Helen Crawford-White for a truly stunning cover.

I'd like to thank the booksellers of Waterstones, Dubray Books, O' Mahonys and Woodbine Books for their fantastic support in the past year.

For the pep talks, encouragement, mentioning my books to other people and listening to my occasional nonsense, I'd like to thank Julian Gough, Gráinne O' Brien, Sarah Moore Fitzgerald and Donal Ryan. A shout-out to the teachers, librarians, fellow writers and other people on Twitter who have been so supportive.

Thanks also to my family, extended family and friends for all your support.

A big thank you to Teagan, the hunter of errant commas.

Special thanks to my agent Sophie Hicks for her advice and for always having my back. I couldn't do this without your help, Sophie. You are a legend.

I love writing for everyone, but it's a special privilege and an honour to write for children, and I'd like to thank all the readers who have spoken to me and written to me in the past year.